Ramshackled

...and 26 other
New England women's
small tales

Mignon Ariel King

Tell-Tale Chapbooks
2016
New England, USA

Ramshackled...and 26 other New England women's small tales
© 2016 Mignon Ariel King

Cover Art: "Girls Night Out" © 2011 Anthony R. Falbo
www.falboart.com

Photo of Author: Todd Collins

Published by

Tell-Tale Chapbooks
New England, USA
http://tell-talechapbooks.weebly.com
making2@outlook.com

ISBN: 9780692417577

In memory of Great Aunt Nina,
whom I never met,
because she loved my mother dearly

He whom love touches not lives in darkness.
~Plato

Part 1: Ramshackled
a novelette about a repurposed life

1 Ramshackled

It was an afternoon that begged to differ. As Allie Kenyon was feeling at odds with *every* thing and everyone anyhow, she decided to take on the angry sky by refuting the importance of its charcoal clouds. Walking out the front door to trip over the left half of a cracked stepping stone on the crumbly-ass front walkway of the highwayside house her eccentric grand aunt had left her, Allie shuffled to the lawyer's office to divest herself of the property, however that was done…to claim indigence and hand over the only thing she had ever been given in this life that meant a dang thing to her. Her parents had left nothing when they went, two weeks earlier, quadruple mortgaging their house and maxing out nearly a dozen credit cards before checking out in a five-car pile-up on the way home from the Cape.

Not once in her life had Ms. Allie M. Kenyon – nee Mary Allison Ramsley – heard her parents agree on or about or with any cursed concept or factual thing, nor with any blessed soul on this green and water-locked Earth, outside of themselves and their perfect daughter Bethany. Then they had died together, instantly, exactly one week after Allie's sister had been put in the ground. Bethany's potted plant had not even been stolen off her grave yet when her parents were laid to rest beside her in the family plot up in Portsmouth, New Hampshire. Allie packed up everything from her parents' curiously Spartan home in less than a week, shredding every scrap of paper outside of the one folder that had something to do with her life. She had left the rest for Big Brothers and the bank to claim then walked past the red and white *For Sale* sign in Newton, Massachusetts. And that was that. Three people toward whom she bore no malice yet to whom she had never been closely connected. Poof! They had emotionally abandoned her decades ago. They had left her to live or die on the streets five years ago. But the Nuclears, as she called them, had still been the last of her blood relatives. She felt like an alien.

It was by sheer luck that Allie had tripped over the blue folder with "Mrs. Nina A. Kenyon" printed on its tab by a label maker sticker. A free spirit who had since the 1940s earned the second paycheck in her marriages from pies and jams, Grand Aunt Nina had been baking ever since she could reach a kitchen table. She had branched out via Nana Nina's Shoppe in her widowhood, selling homemade soaps, handwork, and miniature paintings of her rural childhood via Etsy. "It's a hoot what kinda money rich folks will pay for a bar of soap!" Nana Nina would chuckle. More like a grandmother than a mother's aunt, she had always been called Nana Nina by her grandniece Allie. *Nigh-na, not Knee-na.*

Allie left the lawyer's office a few hours later, stunned. The property was hers outright, totally paid for and with money left over in a trust fund of which Nina's lawyer was the executor. Allie had moved a lot in the five years since her Nana's death, and her inheritance paperwork had been sitting at her parents' house all that time while nobody bothered to inform her. While she lost her condo and lived in her car. While she slept at a shelter where she served as night security guard. While she was medicated into a near-trance to keep from spinning out of control and away for good. Her Nana's house had been there waiting for Allie to snap out of her grief and come home. And those assholes had told her nothing before she had ultimately separated from them forever. Even for the Nuclears, that level of subterfuge and cruelty was astounding to Allie.

Finally, sleeping under the bridge near Kenmore Square had saved her life. Homeless advocates picked her up, dusted her off, and got her into the dorm-like halfway house where a disability check paid for Allie's room and board. Her emergency contact information had brought her sister-friend since grad school zooming to the boardinghouse in Somerville. Juniper had burst through the door with, "Thank God, Sister! You scared hell out of me, disappearing like that. Damned lawyer would not tell me a thing!"

The lawyer had copies of every communication that the Ramsleys had tossed aside or away. They were not bad people, her nuclear family; they simply were not very good people. No official paperwork had ever given anyone custody of Allie. Her parents had been so offended by her imperfection they would not claim her even to control her. They had lied their faces off by omission instead. With absolutely no legal right to make decisions about her or her inheritance, they could not sell the house or rent it, so they simply hadn't bothered to mention it to Allie as they occasionally collected her mail from Walpole and threw it away. "Do what you think is best," is what Lawyer Cam relayed as the Nuclears' rote answer to questions until he gave up communicating with them and did just that. He and Nana Nina had been friends since their semi-rural New Hampshire childhood, reconnecting in "the Big City", having relocated to Massachusetts after WWII. Cam

4

had been a domestic staff sergeant while his brother Ramsey was a gunner who survived a grenade attack on his platoon's foxhole. New Hampshire folks referred to the Commonwealth of Massachusetts as "the Big City," even though Portsmouth was an upper-middle-class town by rural Black people's standards. Their homes had formal parlors in front but also creeks and blueberry bushes in their so-called back yards.

Regardless of rights and ownership, the Ramsleys obviously had had keys and visited the property, checking the pipes and such, putting the lights on timers, and continuing to pay the Carver kid to mow and shovel, slowly throwing away Allie's only adult-life home the way one might work a puzzle for years, just something to do when they were bored. There had been, however, something else afoot. Many of the expensive trappings from the Ramsleys' overstuffed house were boxed and stored in both the house and garage of Nana Nina's Walpole home. Now, under the spotty dark then sunny sky, while everyone else was at work, Allie sneaked into the boarding house where she lived. She hated goodbyes.

Having planned to live at Bethany's condo until her brother-in-law sold it, Allie had already packed up two fat backpacks and tied her futon mattress like a cowboy's bed roll. She used her boarding-house rent money to hire "2 Guyz: 1 Van" off a flyer, insisting that they be there by 2pm. By 2:15 pm, Allie was guiding the van away from Somerville, leading the way to Walpole in her rusty lime-green jeep. She called Bethany's widower Waldo to thank him but no-thank him for the place to crash before swinging by the condo to pick up the few boxes of mementos and artwork that her brother-in-law had packed for her. Waldo had moved back to New York, to his nuclear family, distraught over the loss of his family by marriage. The Ramsleys had adored him. Why not? Like his wife Bethany, Waldo was a perfect specimen of privilege and mainstream success, and he didn't seem to mind the icy civility or champagne-soaked, passive-aggressive spats of his in-laws.

~

It was pouring by the time Allie's books, left half-packed in the living room in Walpole, were run up the human chain of three into the empty second bedroom at the top of the stairs. The room had been totally empty, only the yellow and white wallpaper reminiscent of Nana Nina's former art studio. The 18-year-old version of Allie had moved into the master suite "guest room" on the first floor the summer after high school. She had gone home there on holiday breaks from Portsmouth's Dexter Academy, then from Thoreau College of Communications, and even when Allie lived with a man here and there, the gloriously eccentric house had always been home.

Now her books had the yellow and white studio to themselves, boxed and lining the walls. Apparently her bookcases and white canopy bed set had been thrown out as her parents had progressed halfway through cleaning her room. Part of her wanted to know what in hell they had planned on doing, whether they had disposed of her treasures out of pure spite…but most of her was so relieved to be home that she really didn't care what had happened in her absence. She needed a new sewing machine to replace the one Nana Nina had taught her to sew on, even though the thought of buying something new made her a little dizzy.

It had been a long time since her career ground to a halt via her "episode" and she had walked away from her half of a condo to get away from her fiancé…. Allie avoided the memory. Breathe and focus on the moment…. She unfurled her futon smack in the middle of the floor to do some yoga stretches and lay on it for hours reading *Peanuts Classics, The Big Red Apple,* and *Betty and Veronica* comics. She read and read until the thunder stopped. She had always been petrified by thunder but loved watching the rain splatter and trickle on the huge studio windows in the vaulted ceilings.

In the quiet, Allie walked downstairs, stepping over red-dotted white trash bags, which she discovered contained her former professional wardrobe, to get to the blue-dotted bags of Nana's linens that were mounded about in the half of the living room that had not been stacked with books. Thank God her parents had been the kings of half doing everything. The upstairs was nearly empty except for Nana's bedroom furniture – the naked, cream, queen-sized iron headboard with gold finials, the gold-foiled nightstand, the vanity with mirror, the newer full-length, spinning looking glass Allie had given Nina for Mother's Day, and a chest of drawers. The two black rose and ivory toile chairs that had previously been in the art studio were in the hallway.

Allie smiled, picturing herself curled up in a chair reading while Nana stood at the easel, just six feet away, in a paint-patterned smock. The bangs and feathered sideburns of Nana Nina's short Liza haircut peeked from a purple turban. *Cabaret* boomed from a portable cassette player, drowning out the storm. A large, umbrella-backed floor lamp made the room look sun-splashed. Allie dragged the toil chairs from the second-floor hallway into her new bedroom. Victorian perfection with the pale lavender walls and soft ivory trim that Allie had re-painted six years ago.

The downstairs, Allie soon discovered, was relatively untouched behind and under the books and bags that had been removed from Allie's master suite. The master suite was now crammed full of the Nuclears' treasures, some towers of boxes nearly ceiling high, as if it were a store room. Hidden assets? With Allie's boxed books now upstairs, the living room looked like its old self again under the bags. *The couch!* Allie had not owned a couch since she had broken up with her fiancé five years ago. Since she had broken up with her own self.

Five years ago her Nana had died, and the prick Allie lived with had suddenly decided he wanted kids. Allie left. She left her would-be husband and the investment she had made in their condo. She left her used-to-be career as Director of External and International Communications at a nonprofit. And then she had left her peace of mind...yet again. Allie shook her head to erase the Etch-O-Sketch tableau of her asshole ex-family mumbling about her Nana's death being "for the best." How is it ever best for people who were healthy as horses one day to die the next? Nana Nina died of old age. No disease. No drawn-out illness. She simply wound down and stopped. Allie was happy for her grand aunt, her best friend ever, but sad for herself. She had a right to own her justifiable sadness the way she had owned up to and got help for her bouts of unwarranted sadness and hopelessness once she was old enough to understand that she absolutely was not stupid, lazy, or crazy.

Allie suddenly ran into Nana Nina's kitchen as if she had not just been there that morning. The wooden table with scalloped edges, brought from New Hampshire. The mismatched chair styles, all stripped and painted white with rainbow legs, Allie's own decoupage collages varnished onto their seats. But dearest of all were the seat cushions, with Nina's cross-stitched maxims. "The hurrier I go, the behinder I get." "Judge not, lest ye be judged." "To thine own self be true." "A rolling stone gathers no moss." A fifth and sixth chair had been pulled up to the table. Allie was furious. Those tacky things did not belong there. She opened the designated back door and flung the folding metal chairs onto the screened porch, cursing and slamming the door.

Next, Allie ran around checking all the windows, unlocking then re-locking them three times. She changed the code on the cobweb-covered alarm system – and the red activation indicator blinked on! Whew. All was well again as Allie casually swept an old towel rag over the alarm box then the doorways and baseboards, on her slow way back to the kitchen. The refrigerator was unplugged and emptied but not really cleaned except the top that had just been dusted.

Everything for cleaning was under the sink as before, so Allie scrubbed the kitchen back to normal, impulsively sanding the cupboards with rough paper that was still in the deep supply drawer under the flatware and plastic wrap drawers. Then she retrieved the stick broom, sponge mop, and bucket from the broom closet and cleaned the hell out of the kitchen, scrubbing the Nuclears' touch from the only room they seemed to have used. Allie even mopped the walls with lemon Pine Sol before she plugged in the refrigerator, lemon-purged the powder room, and headed into the living room.

Digging out ivory sheets and blankets, Allie rolled a quilt to use as a pillow and went upstairs to make her bed. The bedroom still smelled of lavender sachets and cedar chips. Allie smiled, feeling her Nana's love in the house rather than the loss of her. The sense of safety and welcome came as a surprise. Allie tentatively crept downstairs and back up several times, hanging her old clothes in her new bedroom, half expecting someone to object. She left all the upstairs windows and closets open while she went to the Stop & Shop to buy food. When the cashier made a joke, Allie bit back her response, counting to five like her therapist had taught her. The cashier was not making fun of Allie's food stamps or her face. "Siobhan" was commenting on the storm, the darkness of the day, and Allie's seemingly excessive purchase. Allie smiled at the girl and handed her twenty dollars for the four boxes of light bulbs on the conveyor belt.

The phone was ringing as Allie walked into the peeling pink with white trim house. She was afraid to answer. Who could it be? She remembered having just come back from The Family Dollar Store and Buffalo Exchange thrift shop. On *that* day. That day when the *Sorry-for-your-loss* ringing had yanked her into the group kitchen, breathless and thunking a frozen ham onto the cheap faux granite kitchen counter in her haste to grab the phone. Nobody else ever used the ground line, kept up by the landlord who lived downstairs. The first thing Allie had thought after hearing of her parents' death that day was that she had spent her last twelve bucks on a XXL sleep tee, crew socks, and a no-name frozen berry tart instead of a bottle of wine. Wrong choice. Instead of a good drunk, she had sat there getting her pie on and drinking a half gallon of chocolate milk.

Here Allie was, feeling the same. Not devastated, but sort of confused by the novelty. She had to get used to being the only living member of three generations of her ever-so-proud New England family. *Pride!* They had pretended she didn't exist ever since the breakdown during graduate school which precipitated the end of her first engagement. Thirty years ago? Something like that. Besides, she had legally changed her last name from her father's following the first time she didn't get married. She simply changed it to her Nana's instead of her would-be husband's. Nana was her family; New Hampshire was her heritage, not Newton, *pool-nobody-swims-in,* Massachusetts. Father had been adopted at birth, so Ramsley was not his father's name anyhow. Who needed it! Father had married up, wayyyyyy up, socio-economically speaking, from his abandoned, nameless, orphanhood. And, oh, the Dickensian love of melodrama with which he had headed up his household.

An abandoned psychiatrist father and a spoiled, socialite, wannabe mother, Allie giggled to herself. No wonder she was so effed up! Allie put a chicken in the oven and set the Miles Kimball ladybug timer. The ding woke her from a nap she hadn't known she was taking, and she smiled. She had never cooked a whole chicken before in her life, but she had helped spoon-stuff hundreds of Thanksgiving turkeys in this very kitchen. She turned off the ringer and ate dinner in front of the huge relic of a television, amazed that a $20 infomercial antenna really worked, feet propped on heaping-trashbags ottoman.

Nana Nina had accepted what she called practicals: a new couch, snow tires for the truck, a refrigerator, and a stove with four consistently working burners instead of two, but she would not hear of a plasma television. *Big Bang Theory* was on channel 38. *Oh!* With a start, Allie realized that her lover Robb had no idea where she was and might be responsible for the ringing telephone. She had completely forgotten he existed. Juniper would call on the smart phone she had handed Allie after the reconnection, stating, "I am *so* not risking losing touch with you again, Girlfriend!" But Allie had just washed down chicken and dark chocolate truffles with a bottle of Barefoot Chardonnay, so she texted her whereabouts to Juniper before stumbling over bags to go upstairs and instantly fell asleep.

2 Just the Facts

Juniper was writing a screenplay, a love story set in the future. The protagonists were deeply in love but in a society in which marriage licenses expired every ten years. A panel of morally correct judges had to pass or fail couples for another ten years' license. Juniper's star-crossed lovers had failed and were living in secret sin, planning to escape to a free love planet before their families could discover the shame. The manuscript was the most bizarre story Allie had read since creative writing workshops in college, maybe high school, but Juniper was the only girlfriend Allie had left as well as a gifted writer who would hopefully work it out ultimately. The sister-friends had met at Thoreau College, where Allie got a Master's in Communications while then-June-now-Juniper was working on a Master's in Fine Arts capstone project. Brilliant, but unfocused. How she ever graduated was a mystery, except for her professor-lover's personal tutelage of course. Juniper was a space cadet who believed in tea leaves and read tarot cards, but she was sweet and loyal, and thank-God-one-hell-of-a-teacher. She taught creative writing at North Shore University.

Juniper still lived with Titian, one of the boys she had shacked up with in Chinatown back in the day. All three of them had lived together as domestic partners, like Mary Wollstonecraft and her ménage à trois. Rafael had married some green-card chick he met at the Dunkin Donuts on Boylston and Tremont ten years ago. Titian insisted that Juniper wear an engagement ring out of fear that some stud would steal her away, but everybody who knew them knew they had zero intention of marrying any time soon, if ever. Compared to the former June and Tito, Allie felt downright boring, but her friends were disgusted by her bigoted, neglectful family. It's good to be around people who think you're the good and normal and decent one in your family melodrama. The couple both thought it horrific that Bethany had called Allie "superfluous," and they asked what argument had brought on that horrible insult. Argument?

Allie had never argued with any of the Nuclears. People have to care about each other to argue. Her flaws were listed, bullet-pointed in the air for her. Her life's task was merely to fix them. She had neglected the To Do list time and time again. Tsk. Tsk. The facts were laid out simply and clearly for her cluttered mind by two psychiatrists, her father and sister. The two affluent, honey-blonde Black people, readily accepted into White high society along with her freckled, strawberry-blonde mother, were clueless about how different bronzed-brown Allie's life was from their own. Add the shame of her lifelong mental health problems, and her family had watched her flee with relief.

Allie was truly sorry for her parents' loss. They had two perfect children once, the strawberry blond son who died from meningitis in kindergarten, and his lovely blonde twin Bethany. Their tragedy was complete, their dotage on the surviving daughter understandable. Then along came Allie, ten pounds of deep brown, slow-learning, finger-painting, different-drummed Allie. Allie had sucked at Math. And Science. And History. Then she started singing in Choir, her grades pulling up just as Father was about to think that even his connections could not send her away to boarding school. Meanwhile, Bethany had cheerleadered and valedictorianed her way to pre-med, following in "Puh-pah's" huge footsteps toward becoming a noted psychiatrist, her beauty landing her a phenomenally handsome divorce-attorney husband and a lucrative radio pop-therapy show that was also podcast. Juniper and Titian called Bethany "Lilith" after *Frasier's* ex-wife. Yet the more they heard about the bitch, the less amusing they found her icy disregard for her very damaged sister.

Allie had never hated her sister; her friends did it for her. Now Bethany was dead. Allie felt guilty for not feeling much…or really anything…about that. The irony. Both the death of her entire nuclear family and their deception were just facts to her. Finally she was being logical and unemotional about something she could not control, but the family who had tried to stomp emotions out of her were not around to revel in the victory.

Allie made a list while waiting for coffee to drip out of the machine, which was red with white polka dots. She had to see the lawyer again to sign her name on deeds and such. She called the phone company to take the bill out of her father's name and decided on impulse to be talked into basic cable television since she wanted Internet service anyhow. The Lifetime Channel awaited. Afraid that she might backslide into an agoraphobic episode, she ordered a grocery delivery for two weeks from tomorrow, a Saturday. She almost cried from a sense of pride when using her Citizen's Bank card to buy food for the first time in five years. Allie had never had a Peapod delivery in life and could not remember the last time she had seen a utility bill with her name on it. She felt like a grown-up.

11

She was an heiress whose lawyer had immediately transferred funds to her checking account? What the wha--? It was almost too much to bear, and she could feel a panic attack coming on. So she paused, put on her black sleep mask with pink and white lace trim, then lay on the couch breathing until her heart stopped pounding.

After a breakfast of multigrain pancakes and Jimmy Dean turkey sausages, cooked on the huge electric griddle just because she had one, Allie went outside to finish her list making for the day. Inside could wait for now. She was set through the Fourth of July weekend even if she did nothing at all. But Juniper and Titian were coming over Sunday for pizza to see if she was up to any exploration and excavation of the premises. Allie could not go into the master suite or basement alone, afraid of feelings and memories, not the dark or the bogeyman. Even on her worst days, she never believed in any of that hooey. A lucky part of her rural inheritance was "good horse sense." If the bogeyman wanted her, he could walk up or down a flight of stairs. Probably was not scared of lights either.

Outside, Allie puttied the broken stepping stone with mud for now while writing "Walkway" on the long, lined shopping list pad of paper that had been magnetized to the fridge. The paper's edges were brown, but she didn't care. Disgraceful that the house had not been painted! She knew for a fact that Nana Nina had scheduled it for 2010. Here it was 2015. "Paint house and garage" went on the list. On impulse, Allie walked down the street, rounded the corner, and jotted down the metal-plated name from the low, white fence she had admired on her grocery run. She especially liked the idea of a gate on the side street rather than on Route 1A – discouraging people from strolling across her dang yard. How hard was it to walk to the corner then turn right onto Kensington Road?

Maybe Sunday she would dare to look in the garage too. The blue pick-up had to be gone, and she couldn't bear to look at the space where it ought to be. Nana Nina had still been driving up until the week before she died. Never had a ticket or an accident in her entire life. Never had anything worse than the flu. No operations. One day, she just wore out. She must have known. They went to say goodbye to New Hampshire, taking turns driving. A week later: *I'm so sorry for your loss.* Now, just like that, Allie sat down on the tree stump with her name carved in it, in her once and current back yard, and started whimpering then crying then wailing.

"Hey, there, Baby Girl?" a voice said, comforting and alarmed simultaneously. It was a distinctly Black and male voice. Two Black

12

folks on the same dead-end street's corner in Walpole at 10am? Allie was surprised out of crying. She sniffled and looked up. The stranger could have been played by Danny Glover in the movie version of Allie's life. He was the least scary total stranger a woman could want standing four feet away on her lawn. And, dang, he seemed familiar. Allie sprang into old-fashioned, raised-right Black lady mode, standing up and reaching over to shake his hand as if welcoming an invited guest into the parlor.

"How do, Neighbor?" Allie said, completely recomposed. "I can't stand weeds!" she joked.

"Ha, haaaa!" the stranger laughed, loud and wide-grinned. "Izzat right? Dandelions getting to a sistah, hunh?"

"Indeed. Hello, I'm Allie," she said as they shook hands. A stunned then pleased look crossed the friendly neighbor's face. He pumped Allie's hand as if she were a former acquaintance he had always wanted to know better...because she was.

"Miss *Allie*? *Nina's* girl? Well, welcome home! I'm Gabe. Gabe Carver, Jr."

"Holy crap! That's who you look like!" Allie burst out. –"Oh, pardon my French. Are you *Welcome's* son?" Gabriel Carver, Sr. had been Nana Nina's close friend, nicknamed "Welcome" by Allie and the other neighborhood kids because of the television show *Welcome Back Kotter*. Like the main sitcom character Gabe Kotter, Gabe Carver, Sr. grew up acting out in school then came back from college to his hometown, employed as the history teacher at Walpole High. His wife, however, had been an architect, not a social worker like Mrs. Gabe Kotter.

"That's right," Gabe said, "your Nana was my Daddy's favorite person on this Earth." Gabe looked exactly like his father except that he had grown salt-and-pepper facial hair. His father always looked like an accountant: clean shaven, navy suit, white shirt with a burgundy tie, Charles Schultzy glasses. Gabe, Jr. had thin-framed tortoiseshell glasses and he wore a pale yellow button-down, khakis, and brown closed-toe fisherman sandals. Allie wanted to sketch him. He was instantly dear to her because of his familiar face, kind voice, and for making her feel special by calling her "Nina's girl." What a happy thought to be known that way, and how good to feel that she had belonged to somebody, been claimed as kin, and was now recognized as such. Welcome home, indeed. Number One Kensington Place, the only house on its own lane.

3 Only Down the Street

"Come on, Miss Allie," Travis asked, "Pleeease, get in the car? You're making a brother feel like Morgan Freeman up in here." Allie slowed her pace to look pointedly at her friend Gabe's son, making it quite clear that she had certainly heard him over the roar of the rain but was choosing not to respond to his pleas. She turned back to her task of staring straight ahead and marching like a woman warrior – about to hunt down lemon-lime seltzer water and liquid egg substitute. Allie had not asked a soul for one darn thing since her Nana Nina had died. Why did Gabe think she was too lame to get her own food now? She tried to concentrate on shrink-wrapped packages of peppers, picturing a red, green, and yellow omelet on her square black plates. She smiled, thinking about the day she had lugged service for 8 into the house for the birthday party.

Nana Nina had been an old-fashioned, transplanted country girl to all outward gazes, but she liked to sprinkle new and "exotic" touches around her mostly French-country-style home, not caring how her mix of styles might look to purists. Nana had dismissed all her dishes with the sweep of an arm one day: "Begone, clutter. I'm done with the Polish stoneware and can't find half my Tupperware. I want squares. Black. And yellow walls? A bumblebee kitchen!" Allie had been so capable then, could have stepped off the cover of *Miznesswoman* magazine. Her Nana had been so proud of her. Now she forgot to buy milk and check the oil in her car. She felt ashamed of forgetting "the mundanities."

As if reading her mind, Travis said, "Ma'am, it's raining like crazy and your car is down. No shame in accepting a little ride. It's only down the street."

"Well, since it's only down the street," Allie said, "I guess even an old broad like me can shuffle down there and back just fine." But she slowed down, confused to be back from her reverie, wondering what the harm could be in receiving a favor. Nana Nina had been a kind soul, always happy to have somebody to love, and she was the only person Allie had ever been herself around, the only person she had dared take favors from until Juniper came along. Over the years she had taken care of her aging grand aunt too until they were simply family and friends, neither the other's caretaker or charge, neither "owing" the other anything but love. Gabriel Senior had been like an uncle, and Gabe Junior felt like a cousin now, so did that make Gabriel Travis Carver III a relative?

Was that what Aunt Nina had left Allie, not just the financial and emotional stability of her family home, but a community to go with it? Allie was upset and just wanted to be home now, but she was physically halfway between two necessities and had a witness. She couldn't lose her cool now.

"You didn't ask for a thing, Miss," Travis's voice centered her. "My Dad did. If you won't get in for your own sake, would you do it for me? Just like your Nana and my Grandpa were friends, you and Dad are friends now. That makes us family." To Travis' surprise Allie stopped completely. Encouraged, Travis went on, "Now, you *know* how my Grandpa got when he didn't get his own way. Dad's just like him. You gonna send me home to tell him I failed at a simple errand he sent me on? Well, hell, why not just shoot me?"

Allie burst into laughter despite herself and walked toward the car. Travis stopped the car and couldn't help being astonished, watching as Allie folded her mini, periwinkle umbrella and her extremely long, bronzed-mahogany legs into the Lexus. As a kid, he had zoomed past her and her grand aunt playing *Monopoly* or poker with his grandfather on the huge screened-in porch. And he had often seen her from a distance over the years. Who hadn't? Even Black folks noticed a six-foot-tall Black woman in Walpole. Just like Miss Nina.

However, Travis had never before seen Allie both up close and wearing neither make-up nor a suit. She was an exact replica of her Grand Aunt Nina, whom she called "Nana." They were two beautiful women who (for reasons he wished he could un-know) had been ramshackled to the job title "Poor Relations" – while their equally beautiful sisters had led lives of extreme social privilege and haughty hatefulness toward their supposedly natural inferiors.

Travis knew it was wrong to speak ill of the dead, but he couldn't help thinking that Allie's sister and parents had been three of the worst human beings he'd ever heard of. His best friend Benny called them "rat bastids"…Gahd rest their souls…raaaat bastids." Well, yeah, that about summed it up.

~

Allie was home from Stop & Shop with a refrigerator full of food, bathed and eating eggs with Pillsbury biscuits and a glass of Frey's white table wine, two hours after discovering that the walk-through butler's pantry was half full of Nana Nina's boxed things and half full of the Nuclears' stuff. Interesting. Allie vaguely recalled hearing something about a broken pipe in her parents' basement a few years ago, when she had called her sister and spoken to Waldo because she had lost her birth certificate. Yeah, right – they probably took a sledgehammer to the pipe themselves if indeed there was a leak at all…if indeed two highly intelligent people had stored valuables in their basement instead of the bone-dry, remodeled attic. Ignorance was bliss as far as Allie was concerned. Whatever they had been up to, she didn't need to know. But she also did not want their stuff anywhere near her home. So she had decided to have a yard sale then paint the entire kitchen, dining room, and powder room. She didn't want a yellow kitchen though.

Digging a path through the boxes that morning, Allie had found kitchenware that she had packed during the showdown the month after her grand aunt's death, five long years ago. Stella had casually mentioned her plans for emptying her aunt's house, and Allie had *lost* it. Screaming at her parents to back off, Allie had scared them away long enough to pack many items of sentimental value on the first floor, including the black square dishes, grey-topped food storage tubs, carbon steel and brushed stainless steel small appliances – the entire kitchen she had bought as a surprise for Nana Nina's last birthday party. They had feasted on Japanese food with Juniper, Titian, Allie's fiancé Charles, and Nana Nina's oldest girlfriend, Marie, all sitting around in kimonos drinking sake and laughing. The next day, the surprise had been on Allie when Nina swept her away to New York for four days of fun. Allie was flabbergasted when Nina told her she'd been "socking away some cash in the ol' mattress" for years to celebrate her 80th birthday in style.

It turned out that the frugal old woman had been making a modest fortune from her online business and stashing it in a joint bank account. Her will and the trust fund had both Allie's chosen and given names as beneficiary. "Nee Mary Allison Ramsley" raised a toast to Mrs. Nina Alice Kenyon, "DBA Nana Nina's Shoppe," wearing an authentic amethyst kimono dug out of a 30-gallon plastic tub. Then Allie began a list for the yard sale and fell asleep on the couch, a fleece throw blanket up to her chin, a fire in the hope-it's-up-to-code fireplace, and HGTV on the new plasma that sat atop the 1950s television which served as a TV table. The *Property Brothers* would be horrified.

16

Gabe and Travis were going to help Allie begin to clear the house of both Nina's castoffs and the Nuclears' ill-gotten gains, dragging everything into the garage for the impending yard sale. *Shit. What are the chances there's a lock on that garage door?*

Allie pulled herself into the now, breathing a sigh of accomplishment. She had hauled the supplies to re-do the kitchen, dining room, and powder room in three hues of blue and cream or ivory with paint gathered from Craigslist leftovers, the South Shore Homeowners' Cooperative, and the Home Depot before her car had clonked out. Juniper and Titian were coming for Fourth of July dinner, sleeping over after spending the day on phase two of excavating the big old house. Allie wanted to paint the inside of the house while the workers remade the outside over the course of the upcoming week.

4 I Never Met a Potato I Did Not Like.

1929: New Hampshire to 2015: Walpole, Massachusetts. Every memento of Nina A. Kenyon's life and that of her grandniece and unofficial charge Allie M. Kenyon, once dotted behind or in front of her niece Stella's cache, breathed easy in the now-weeded kitchen. The first row of Stella and Sterling's stash had been tossed about, almost littered, in a semi-circle in the basement, as if someone had frantically searched for then found something and just walked off. A Tiffany lamp sat on a folding table next to two tan, padded folding chairs that matched the pair Allie had flung from the back door off the kitchen. Nina's painted-to-be-a-set chairs remained in the kitchen, but Allie had re-painted the rings a dusty blue and the table a soft creamy white, remaining very busy for the past week until her friends were on vacation for July and could help.

It was 8 p.m. Saturday, dinner time. An exhausted trio of friends were waiting for their pizzas. A red, white, and blue ice cream cake waited in the refrigerator. Allie was emotionally wrung out, so she bought some extra alone time in the upstairs bathroom to reflect on the decluttering of the basement and garage. Juniper and Titian, who didn't have a modest bone between them, were showering then changing in the living room. Thank goodness for curtains. Allie had smashed down the wall separating the kitchen from the family room, so there was only a peninsula counter bisecting the largest common area now. The small eating nook against the back wall of the kitchen looked cozy again rather than cramped, and it was the only place to eat, the dining room containing only the large French Country cream hutch and tremendously heavy table that no one could remember having ever not been in there. The dining-room chairs, rug, and lights were gone, even the chandelier.

Allie was trying hard, but she was still reeling from the initial shock of discovering that the Nuclears had used her home as a storage facility for sneaky reasons she only half comprehended. What she did know for certain is that she had spent five years spiraling down the drain she had circled tight for her entire life, but especially for twenty years. Five years of crashing in spare rooms, attics, and basements at best, couches, her car, then shelters at worst. She had lost her Nana, career, and condo, then lost her grip entirely. And her home had housed nothing but material wealth.

The Ramsleys had left everything to Bethany, which maybe included debts, but then Bethany had died first. Legally, Allie was

18

not responsible for any of their mess and swore it all off just as they had cast her and her issues aside. So she was feeling zero moral dilemma over glomming their treasures and Nana Nina's Goodwill piles together, selling it all for cold, hard cash, and putting the hodgepodge behind her. She needed a new car. She needed food twelve months per year. She needed a fresh start in a cohesive and uncluttered home to cobble her life back together. *Uncertainty about her new life did not bother her. It was the past that gave her fear.* She had a new word, part of Nana Nina's legacy. Hope. Where was the *Dum Spiro Spero* framed sampler? She was just about to cry wondering about it when the bell rang.

"Could you get that...if you're decent?!" Allie called downstairs. "There's cash in the entryway drawer!"

"We ain't decent, but we're dressed! No worries!" Titian called back. Allie smiled, happy to have her closest friends and her home united. It was surreal, morphing now into normal. *Mmm, pizza,* she thought. She needed something positive and current to focus on, and a sudden gnawing hunger was just as good as anything. It is curious that losing one's mind takes up just as much energy as cultivating it.

Now that she was on an emotional plateau, Allie could focus for a bit on organizing her future work project before the next wave of crazy hit. But what exactly her future work would be wasn't as yet clear to her. If she were a cook or a painter, a writer, a soap maker...a poet or a preacher – the '70s tune popped into her brain and she just let it ride for a bit before refocusing on what to focus on next in life. Having always worked for a living, she couldn't conceive of project work minus someone else's deadlines. But she did know that hers was a mind that required tasks, deadlines, and outcomes. She would make work for its own sake, for her own sanity, not just for employment. It was a liberating and frightening concept. For once karma was a lady instead of a raging bitch. Allie had bought the double oven, state-of-the-art useful yet cute as Minnie Mouse's kitchen for Nana Nina's baking business and pleasure. And now Allie had a beautiful kitchen to enjoy as she relearned and remembered everything her grand aunt had taught her there. 52 and taking baby steps. But at least she felt like stepping, God bless.

Allie didn't think Nana Nina would mind if the first dessert Allie made in five years was a no-bake banana torte. Sunny had made one on *The Rachael Ray Show*. Nana had watched it, so...an idea popped into her head and she thought it would help to have a TV in

19

the kitchen to use as a guide/company. *Oh, good thinking, kiddo. Write that down.* She did just that.

Dressed, head wrap removed, Allie followed the smell of pepperoni and sausage with onions into the kitchen. It had been odd when Titian and Juniper appeared on her doorstep. Out of context. Yet she'd flung open the turquoise door with great flair and said, "Welcome to my humble abode."

Now Allie walked into her own kitchen as if visiting her friends' instead. Titian hopped from the kitchen island stool and gushed, "Oh, Allie! Your hair is indeed marvelous!" He had noticed a few curls peeping out of Allie's orange head wrap, assessed that it might be a flattering look, and now announced that his findings had indeed been correct. Titian often spoke as if others were privy to the inner monologues leading up to his shared pronouncements.

"Thanks!" Allie said, turning her coiled head side to side for Juniper's opinion as Titian tested one springy twist.

"I love it. I honestly love it." Juniper proclaimed, grandly but sincerely. Allie began to hum and the trio burst into a verse of Olivia Newton John. *Maybe I hang around here a little more than I should...!* Juniper's own hair was about an inch long, growing back from a near-scalp-shining buzz cut. She wore long dangling earrings that looked like pink-beaded curtains suspended from tiny clothes hangers through her ears. Her white tunic flowed over pink leggings that disappeared into open-toed black ankle boots with gold zippers up the heels. She wore no other jewelry except her engagement ring.

Allie was the fashion opposite of Juniper, having grown out the last of the short, chemically-relaxed styles that had been her trademark for her entire career. She'd been wearing hats or scarves for five years now, styling her hair being the least of her concerns. On an impulse one night, Allie had sat twisting her hair while watching TV. She had always been good with hair and make-up and joked that she had put the Fashion Fair president's kid through college. Her features both strong and lovely, she could wear a lot of make-up quite well. Now her cheeks and eyelids were bronzer; just a hint of frosted caramel glossed her lips. She wore a "recycled" lilac and aqua striped '60s midi dress with high-heeled silvery sandals. Her wrists were stacked with silver and wooden cuffs, adorned with turquoise and embedded shells. The three middle fingers on her right hand were beringed: silver filigree, an elongated black wooden

20

African mask, and a totem of sterling skulls. She wore wooden mask posts in her ears and five strands of ivory pearls interspersed with a few strands of turquoise stones. It would have been too much on an average-sized woman, but six feet and three inches of Allie looked somehow regal and fun, as if regular clothes were downright unworthy. Yet, when employed Allie had been the poster girl for New Englander normal clothes, looking like one of the models in Eddie Bauer catalogs…until 5p.m. She always looked like a square or an *It* girl, no in-between.

Sitting in her *It* kitchen with her two oldest and dearest friends, Allie felt blessed and incredulous, half-afraid she was having some bizarre "episode" and had created a world in which she did not live in a homeless shelter with five strangers waiting for housing that would never come and being forgotten by most of her good-time-Charlie friends. Friends from work. What an oxymoron. She had never seen work friends on weekends and rarely saw her lovers on weekdays. The only constants had been Nana Nina, Juniper, and Titian. And in a way, they were all still here, reunited by the house.

"You okay, Allie?" Juniper asked.

Allie had wolfed down two slices then sat silently in front of an empty plate thinking for longer than she had realized. "I'm fine," she said before uncharacteristically sharing what was in her head. "I didn't think I'd ever see this room again. I can't believe you two are here. And I miss Nana Nina so much less now that I'm in her home again. I thought it would be the opposite."

"Right?" Juniper confirmed. "I feel happy, like she brought us lost sheep back to the fold by leaving you the house. She knew this is your home and where your community is *supposed* to be hanging out. And you re-did it to perfection!" Allie had cleared out the kitchen, keeping everything blue, white, black, or stainless steel and boxing the rest up on the back porch for Boomerangs. Paint the top half of the room blue and the wainscot a creamy ivory. Lay down a black floor. Done. She had been so afraid to start, so confused about what to do. She had wanted to preserve and honor without dwelling on sadness, as the saying on the wall over the nook advised. Allie had wanted to start over without feeling like a foreigner. She had fretted and fretted. Then Gabe had come to the rescue yet again, just as he had that day Allie was crying on the tree stump.

"Gabe said he didn't think Nana Nina would mind if I redecor- ated, that she would say it's my house so I can paint it whatever the heck colors I want. Do you think it *is* okay?" Allie polled her friends.

"Girl, it's always been your home too. Hell, no, Miss Nina wouldn't mind. She would've asked for your input when she repainted anyhow," Titian exclaimed. "Are you feeling survivor's guilt or something? Cuz knock that shit the hell off. Miss Nina was all about living and making people happy. You want to honor her memory? Damn, Girlfriend, be happy! It's okay to enjoy breathing!"

Allie burst into tears and Juniper ran over to hug her.

"Oh. My. God! I said the exact wrong thing? Me and my mouth," Titian said. Allie and Juniper both smiled at him in the secret men-are-morons way women do.

"No, Honey..." Juniper began to explain.

"...you said the *exact* right thing!" Allie finished. "Thank you! Guilty is exactly how I was feeling. Spend five years whining and glumming without her to take care of me. Now she's taking care of me from beyond, giving me back my home and my people, and I was feeling like an ingrate for painting a freakin' kitchen. Once you said it, it sounded so silly. She loved me. She left me the house so I could be housed and fed and as happy as humanly possible. It's my duty to get my happy juices going."

"Happy juices?" Titian asked, flipping the mood to ask, "More wine?" The trio laughed at their own weirdass little family and had a toast.

"What color for the outside?" Juniper asked when the friends were seated on the couch that was back-to the kitchen. Where there had once been a wall, only the satiny black wood of the floor and a small island were between them and the kitchen nook.

5 Ends

It was Tuesday and the painters were slathering away outside, where it was mercifully sunny but not godawful hot or sticky for the second week of July in Massachusetts. Allie had painted light teal vertical stripes on the freshened-cream paint of the dining room walls and was toying with the idea of concurrent thin gold or maize stripes to break up the cuteness of the powder blue and cream that had spilled over from the kitchen. She had not inherited any fine arts painting or sketching skills from her mother's side of the family, but she had an eye for quiet elegance. Thinking it a good idea to get out of the paint-fumed house for a while, she had walked to Walpole Center to read magazines at the public library then sip an iced vanilla latté at the small mom and pop's café.

As Allie was leaving the café, the bus was leaving the Center. For the first time in over twenty years Allie decided to take public transportation to a destination other than the airport. She flagged down the bus and boarded, having no clue as to where she was going. A car-free field trip was better than sitting in the house trying not to peek at the exterior's progress. She had left sweet tea and lemonade on the now-front porch for the smiling workers with whom she had conversed in flawless Spanish. Allie also knew enough French and German to get by on past vacations to Europe.

She had hopped off at the first sign of major commerce and happily ended up at a large TJ Maxx in Dedham. She needed some new pajamas. Having slept at "The Asylum," then the shelter, then the boarding house – and planning to sleep in her car again for a bit – Allie had longed for the formality of sleepwear rather than her all-purpose sweats. But it had not seemed worth spending any of her disability checks on. Her parents had footed the inpatient stay, per usual; they had no problem helping to hide Allie. It was the helping her get or feel better part that stumped them. The Ramsleys had not planned on improvement or a thriving life ever happening, and they did not mind letting Allie and "idealistic" Nina know that they considered Allie's psychiatric stability a lost cause.

She had lingerie at Robb's house. Robb was financially generous, yet Allie had an entire second life and personality that he did not know or care to know. She was too damaged to be fully embraced into his methodical life. That lack of emotional support was reason enough to ignore the demands of a ringing ground line.

Allie had no room in her brain for him right now. The half-assed romantic relationship made her sad; her lover knew her about as well as her former work friends did. Faking normal with him had been exhausting, and going from luxury to the boardinghouse hurt.

Sad had been part of Allie's life for so long that it had not previously occurred to her to challenge it rather than merely weather its waves until they quieted down. Then lonely had moved in for five long years. She was sick of both feelings. Allie's weight had yo-yoed from all the medicine she had been hopped up or zoned out on before meeting a feminist doctor with some dang sense. Dr. Markus had tapered her off to one medium-dose antidepressant and bi-weekly behavioral therapy. Slowly but surely winnowing down to her normal weight had inspired Allie to begin exercising again. Now size XL clothing hung off her.

Allie held a short nightie and robe set to her front and admired herself in the store mirror, but she quickly put it back when she drew an audience of the only two men in the store. Twenty dollars? Seriously?! Her last nightwear trip had been down Newbury Street. She had not been a budget kinda girl in her most financially stable years, but after five seemingly endless years of financial instability that matched the other upset in her inner and material life, Allie was flabbergasted that she could actually buy *food* she liked. So seeing clothing that was both attractive and within her new budget was unbelievable.

Unsurpisingly, discounted pajama sets were too short for her six-foot frame, so Allie resignedly plodded toward the men's section. No men's pajamas? This was turning into a bummer of an excursion until Allie turned to leave and saw them. Two gorgeous, sumptuous, jewel-toned deep teal chairs, with an embossed, not-quite fleur-de-lis pattern. They were up on a dais with a matching pair on the sales floor behind them along with an assortment of other chairs. Their slight, curving wings and plush seats were studded with burnished silver. Just enough silver. The mahogany legs were simple, straight lines, stained black. Half-afraid to look, Allie reached them in three giant steps then gasped in disbelief. $129.00 each. Cynthia Rowley. On the table on the display sat two Simon Blake lamps in a distressed light teal that matched the striped wall Allie had just created. $40.00 each. *Sold!* She had just redecorated the entire first floor for less than a thousand dollars if she made cushion covers for the kitchen nook herself. Free paint remnants, glass mosaic backsplash tiles, and welcome mats from

24

Craigslist had saved the day.

Allie caught her breath as she felt a panic attack begin. She sat in one of the chairs, breathing out. Then she pulled out her cell before she had a chance to talk herself out of placing a call.

"Hello…Miss Allie?" Gabe answered. He had made certain she had his number after sending Travis for the grocery run, with a *call-anytime-don't-be-shy* directive.

"Hi, Gabe," Allie said. "I'm at the TJ Maxx."

"Baby Girl, what are you doing way down in Dedham? Need a lift back?" Gabe asked.

"Funny you should ask," Allie laughed. "I'm about ready to chain myself to four dining room chairs here because I can't take them all in a cab."

"I'm on my way to a job, but hold on," Gabe said with a chuckle. Allie could hear his voice rumbling then clearing back into intelligible sound, "Dorothy would love to come carry you back if you don't mind."

"Mind? Wouldn't that be a huge imposition?" Allie said in a worried tone.

"Not at all. She's about to be abandoned for dinner and would love the company," Gabe explained. And just like that, Allie and Dorothy were riding down Route 1A, Allie insisting that Dorothy stay for dinner if she didn't mind the semi-mess.

"I'm an attorney," Dorothy said. "We're used to messes!" She was lovely in an apricot sweater set and jeans with sparkly tan ballet flats. Her jet-black hair was Halle Berry short, bangs spiked for her afternoon off. Her friendly, curious eyes and huge dimples had been passed on to her son Travis, while her twinkly-eyed daughter Diana favored Gabe. An emergency had called Gabe to Framingham. A burst pipe repair after 6pm was a plumber's dream. There was no telling what time he'd be back, so Allie really did feel that her company was welcome. She had practiced not being in people's way for so long that she had difficulty distinguishing between actual interest in her as a specific individual versus a generalized human kindness. *Mean* she recognized right off. She had interacted with a lot of mean people in this life.

The new girlfriends ordered Chinese food and sat on the dining room furniture they had just lugged back from the Dedham Mall. Dorothy complimented the fresh pitcher of sweet tea as well as Allie's striped walls. Allie smiled, picturing the two of them on the now-cream and-charcoal, screened-in front porch where Nana Nina

25

and Welcome had spent many summers. The old wicker set had six chairs which were sitting in Allie's sewing room after receiving a new coat of ivory spray paint. Four chairs would be returned to the front porch along with the now-lime-green wicker couch and black, lady-bug-dotted pillows. The two former back-porch chairs could easily be moved around. Trying now to put together a decent wardrobe for her post-career life, she needed a chair upstairs in her bedroom. Eventually the chair might end up upstairs in the library. Allie's new sewing room was on the first floor at the back of the house; she could look out at Rte. 1A through the new fence which would prevent her feeling as though the entire world were frowning back at her. The room used to be storage, as the house had no attic and a tiny, cold basement for such a large house. The attic had been knocked down decades ago, raising the second floor ceiling so that every bit of natural light possible could stream into Nina's art studio windows around the knarled, stained mahogany support beams.

Allie hadn't been to a mall with a girlfriend in years. Juniper was a great thrift shop fan like Allie, but Juniper had zero interest in "mainstream" clothes. So Allie had truly appreciated being gently prodded by Dorothy into the Old Navy. There she found three pair of jeans that actually fit. Dorothy was a shopping expert. Allie's comment about her original quest for "normal ol' comfy pajamas" was rewarded with turquoise, lilac, and ivory satin sets before the mall trip had concluded. It would be days before Allie wore her new clothes, it was so satisfying to look at the shopping bags sitting on the wicker chair next to the full-length looking glass in her lilac and cream bedroom. She did not have a favorite color, but Nana Nina had loved every shade of pink and purple, so Allie left the bedroom as she'd found it except for washing the walls and floor during painting breaks the previous week. Her Nana had always called her "an old farm girl." Proudly. Nina had stayed in her childhood home in Franklin, New Hampshire until her parents died. It was a fluke to meet her first husband at her niece Stella's Christmas party, but a well-timed fluke. Nina's sister, also named Stella, had been incensed by the class difference, but Nina had not hesitated to accept a marriage proposal and "move on up to the big city" aka Boston, Massachusetts. Nana Nina's first husband had died of a heart attack in his sleep. Then along came her second and final husband, the love of her life. Uncle Jerome, a carpenter, had been wonderful. All he and Nina ever did was laugh, like the best friends that they were. Then Nina had inherited Jerome's best friend since middle school, Welcome Carver.

Dorothy's voice brought Allie back to the present. "More broccoli?"

"Yes, please," Allie said. The two had made a formal dinner party out of christening the finished room. With the new lamps on the old sideboard and the lushly upholstered chairs adding a regal touch to the room under the huge, three-tiered, 1950s crystal chandelier brought in from the entryway, the room was picture perfect. It seemed almost silly *not* to use the cloth napkins and hand-painted rings that had sat untouched for five years in the sideboard's drawers. Take-out cartons and paper napkins would have been an insult to the reawakening spirit of friendship and laughter that had made the house a legend in its neighborhood. The square black plates on the ivory tablecloth of Allie's college holidays sealed the marriage of old and new, simple and grand.

"I *do* wish I could add a photo of this to Nana Nina's cookbooks," Allie said.

"Why can't you?" Dorothy asked, feeling sorry when Allie's face dropped. Dorothy quickly added, "If you finish her last book it could be a tribute to her." That worked. Allie brightened.

"I never thought of that! I typed the text, you know? It's still saved in my Gmail with the jpeg images. I could write a last chapter, like an epilogue, with the recipes she didn't get to and photos of the redecorating she had planned!" Allie practically exploded with enthusiasm and ideas. "Oh, I'm sorry. I'm getting worked up and have had too much wine."

"Don't apologize," Dorothy said. "I think it's a great idea...for her fans and for you...and for Nana Nina. I hear she did not like to leave things unfinished."

"No. No, she did not!" Allie agreed. "And I think I can recreate some of the missing recipes, though I'm no great cook." She wanted to ask if Dorothy, a phenomenal soul food goddess, would help, but she didn't know how.

"I'd love to help!" Dorothy laughed. "I was a fan too, ya know? I have all of her books. Northern and Southern sisters, let's come together!" She impulsively hugged Allie who was surprised to find herself hugging back. Travis was right. The Carvers were Allie's family.

"Thank you!" Allie was beaming. By the time Gabe arrived to pick up his wife, Dorothy had photographed the kitchen and dining room and Allie in two outfits, and the girlfriends had written a To Do draft for August on the kitchen fridge list, mapped around Dorothy's work schedule and Allie's therapy appointments.

"Wow!" Gabe laughed on the porch, scooping his tipsy wife in with one arm as if she were about to topple over. "Leave two sistahs alone for a half day and they buy out all the malls, reorganize the world, and apparently drink all the wine in New England." He fanned the air as if it reeked like an alley. He was wearing the traditional blue coveralls of plumbers of yore.

"You stop that, Gabe Junior!" Dorothy giggled.

"Hey, at least we saved you some," Allie defended, handing him a corked, half-bottle of pink zinfandel and a small recycled Whole Foods bag full of still-cartoned food.

"Oh, yes you did! Redemption!" Gabe laughed.

After her friends had gone, Allie loaded the dishwasher then looked at the pretty kitchen before shutting off the light. She went in for a last look at the dining room too, thinking she would now add skinny silver stripes to go with the chair studs and increase the blueness of the room when she got around to it. She fingered the silver locket around her neck, smiled at the thought of making her sewing room yellow- and black-striped, with stenciled bumble bees in honor of Nana Nina's yellow kitchen. Maybe at Christmas. Passing the master suite, her former bedroom, Allie kissed her locket, whispered, *Thank you. I love you.* She pictured the face smiling back at her through the tiny hinged cover. Then she climbed the stairs with her shopping-bagged treasures and went to bed.

6 Feed People. They *Will* Come Back.

Allie sat in the upstairs library unpacking books onto the shelving delivered that morning. She listened to digging and pounding as half the fence was being built, then she walked to Walpole Center for a sandwich while the other half of the fence was being installed. She spent hours sketching clothes, curtains, and pillow covers for the dining nook, first in the sandwich shop then in the public park. The stroll up had been fun and refreshing, but walking back had made her increasingly more agoraphobic until she picked up the pace and hurried home for suppertime. Heat, bugs buzzing, the sawing and calling out of workmen, and the sudden crowds of employed people commuting home from Boston had assaulted her new-found sense of calm. The stench of a newly constructed house's yard being dug up had overpowered the sweet smell of flowers yearning over low fences or sprawling unfenced in rural-style yardscapes. Allie retreated home, fantasizing the entire time about finishing the powder room so she would have a positive image to focus on. She needed to relax, maybe start sewing soon.

She stopped abruptly on the corner of Rte. 1A and Kensington Road. The house was perfect. The five-foot black metal fence framed the sage house with charcoal grey shutters without blocking any natural light. Walking stones led from the highwayside back door to the first Kensingston gate, brightening the red maple that reigned over the left side of the back yard. Even with the repositioned walkway (which would now be curved to the left rather than straight), the reclaimed back of the house would be inviting enough for the cook-out yard sale that Allie was planning. Everything that she, Juniper, and Titian had pulled out, loosely repacked, and returned to the garage was tagged. Allie couldn't wait to get rid of the Nuclears' crap. Aside from not wanting to look at their leftovers or have their valuables kicking around in case it was all hidden as some financial slight-of-hand, Allie was going to buy an SUV to replace her car and Nana Nina's pick-up. The yard sale money would come in handy. Relieved and pleased to have done so much, Allie was excited to have no housekeeping duties to do for August except prepare for the yard sale. She was still confused at the thought of relaxing for a month. Nothing to do but sew, work out, and edit Nana Nina's last book.

Tackling the rest of the master suite, packing up her former wardrobe for consignment, and especially seeing what was left of her childhood belongings, was too much for right now. Juniper had suggested they put it off until Labor Day weekend. Allie could have hugged her out of relief. She was getting acclimated to living on the second floor and feeling happy. Her old room threatened to be full of too much used-to-be. Allie had no room in her mind for "used-to-be a professional" right now and did not care to go through her closet. Was it empty or full of more suits? Were any of her shoes left? She hoped some part of her childhood mementos survived, once pressed behind her relatives' relics, but she was also too frightened to look now that the door opened all the way again. The towers of newer boxes had contained off-season clothing and such, but one look at the improvised storehouse that used to be her refuge was enough to cause a horrific sobbing fit. It would never be the same. She had closed the door.

The dining room, former pie room, and powder room had been completely cleared except for the dining table and sideboard; Allie's suite was next, counterclockwise. So her suite was either stripped like the upstairs and back rooms or untouched like the living room and kitchen. Maybe more linen, boxes of fabric and notions, and curtains were in some boxes; maybe they were all gone. She had stopped scolding herself for not wishing to know yet. She had to keep herself together long enough to meet her new neighborhood. New neighbors had moved in all around, interspersed with townies her age who remained in their deceased parents' or grandparents' homes rather than selling.

Nina's pies had kept feeding the neighborhood even after her professional staff near Egleston Square in Roxbury had taken over the mass production and freeze-packing of all the home goods sold via her Internet empire. She had named her "home goods and good home eating" *Nana Nina's Shoppe* after branching out; however, she had still baked pies in her kitchen for pleasure and sold them to neighbors at a fraction of the business price, a mere $6.00.

Allie's mother Stella had been just as scandalized in Massachusetts as Grandmother Stella had been in New Hampshire that Nina cooked for White people. It was shameful and servile to them, not entrepreneurial. Nina had laughed at that. "Ha," she said, "Stella the star, with her butterscotch hair, marries a White man then dictates how *I'm* selling out to 'the Man' by earning a living and a community doing what I love. Too buppity for her own good, sitting on her plastic duff with her faux friends."

Nina had paused, hand shooting to cover her mouth. Then she

declared, "I am so sorry, Child. I forget sometimes."

"It's okay," Allie had laughed out, "I forget sometimes too…or at least try to! Prodigal me, the blackest of sheep." The White man Stella married was of course Allie's father, Sterling. He had changed his name on his college application, preferring its sound. Eventually Dr. Sterling S. Ramsley gave his birth name, Seymour, to his infant son. Then he'd had the nerve to pitch a fit when his daughter Mary Allison had changed her name to Allie Marie. The one time he might have understood her and connected somehow, Sterling had bellowed at the top of his lungs and sent Allie running from her nuclear home to her emotional home for life. All Allie had taken with her was the clothing she liked – leaving the "suitable" garb Stella and Bethany had crammed into her closet. She had sneaked back in to pack twenty boxes of books and filled sketchpads, packing them into Nina's pick-up.

At 18, Allie had spent most of her life at boarding schools and country-home-feeling psychiatric facilities anyhow. She had driven to Nana Nina's and never really left for good, going to college and graduate school in Massachusetts, sometimes living in dorms or with boyfriends, sometimes living in Nina's first-floor guest suite. Nina had loved young people and was always happy to have a house full of college girls listening to music, dancing, helping with and eating her never-ending supply of homemade food. Allie had become a pretty good cook, but sewing skill was her trademark. She had loved lace and ruffles, color and pattern. Eff "tasteful neutrals" in her personal life. Both her nuclear-relative psychiatrists and her hired professionals had labeled her flirtatious and oversexed. Allie had never flirted in her life. Oversexed, she would gladly cop to. But only because she was a girl. Nobody would call a single male "oversexed" due to premarital enthusiasm for the opposite sex. Outside of her family dynamic, she was often considered beautiful. Men asked her out. She loved men. She would date a man until he annoyed her then move on.

Allie pulled her focus back to the current month of August. She had created a roundabout way of finding women friends. A yard sale to get rid of the Nuclears' cache of goods, with free pie to entice potential buyers into socializing as well as to test her memories of Nana Nina's recipes. With any luck, some customers would become her friends. As Nana Nina had always said, "If you feed people, they'll come back!"

7 There's Always One Fly

Red and white checkered paper tablecloths for strawberry and cherry. Yellow with pink daisies in every other square for lemon meringue and banana crème. Blue and white for blueberry. And green for sweet potato. These had been Nana Nina's color-codings for pies left cooling on the front porch when it served as a storefront, way back in the days when the house still had a dark, perilous-floor-planked attic. With prosperity and a second husband who had knocked out the top floor and added huge support beams to create a sun-splashed second-floor studio for Nana's artwork and had built pie safes in the game room, the house had cheered itself up and enveloped the 18-year-old outcast Allie. Now Allie presided over the cutting of free pie at her most interactive event since quitting her career. The yard sale was a hit. She let a few items go for $10.00 or so, having hoped they would fetch more, but it had taken all her will power not to gasp when some items went for hundreds.

A hideous frame from The Nuclears' stash in the garage went for $700.00. That which looked like faux rococo to Allie caused a bidding war between two serious treasure hunters who had actually driven all the way from Boston's Back Bay area and from Medford. The Medford bidder had bought an antique store in Brookline Village and was preparing to move to the living space above it. He proudly hauled away the mirror, grateful for Allie's help, and left her staring in disbelief at the stack of new bills. Allie brought out two of Nina's smaller paintings, one of cows at sundown and one of a black horse under a purple night sky and sliver of moon, as a consolation prize for Christopher Dawes. After purchasing the bucolic pair for $800.00 and a smitten sigh, Christopher became Allie's and Juniper's new old friend. He lived with his surgeon partner on Commonwealth Avenue and worked at an art gallery on Newbury Street. He went around inspecting the high-end goods, retagging with a whispered, "Sister, not even close. Not even."

So it was done. The last person to turn Allie's parents' junk into coveted treasure turned left onto the highway toward Westwood with a Tiffany's-style floor lamp and one whole banana crème pie she had insisted on paying for. Allie had boxed it, tied it with string, and even added a "Nana Nina's Shoppe ~ Pies Since 1960" sticker from the game/pie/yoga room butcher-block drawer. Exhausted but relieved and proud to have pulled it off, Allie kicked off her shoes and slouched into the couch, polling her friends.

"Who's staying for pizza. And who wants meat?" Allie asked.

"Ooh, sausage and onion with extra cheese?" Christopher was raising his wrists together under his chin like a begging puppy.

"Oh, see, now I knew we were vibing," Allie praised. "Cheese for you, Juniper and Dorothy? Hawaiian for Titian and Wendy?" Wendy was a new neighbor-friend. Her sister Rhianna had gone home to walk the dog, but she was obviously now one of the gang. A chorus of *yeses* later, Allie had begun ordering the food on the phone when the doorbell rang. Allie frowned, counting friends.

"Omigod, how did Allie know what kind of pizza I want?" Wendy asked. She was 40ish, but she omigod-ed a lot and seemed much younger overall. She had talked all afternoon about college in California as if she had just graduated that summer. Maybe someday everyone would find out what she did for a living and if she had finally made up her mind between her "ex" and her current boyfriend. For now, they knew about the – she meant *the* best pizza and sushi ever. Conversation was cut short as Allie handed the phone to Juniper and went with a slight trepidation in her walk to answer the door. Christopher instantly noticed Allie's hesitation and that she was silently counting; he popped off the couch.

"Shall I come with?" Christopher offered. He was rewarded by a nervous, grateful smile. The two went to the door. Less than a minute later, the mumbled conversational tones turned angry to the group inside. Everyone rushed to the porch, shocked to find Allie's next-door neighbor hopping mad with a bright red, rage-contorted face.

"That's my fucking property!" the livid Mitchell Bale shrieked, punctuating the air with a finger jab in the direction of Allie's front-yard fence. The eight free Craigslist trees just stood, firred in green silence alongside the fence. Bale had been on vacation for the summer. Allie's entire life had changed...she had become a real person; she had a home again and her old friends and new ones too; she had let go of things that no longer served her needs; she had decided to try again...and she had slowly emerged to repurpose her empty hours all while someone else was on vacation. Her coming back home, back to life, had inconvenienced him? Maybe it was true. So she'd move the fence. So what?

Allie blurted out, "So, what if you're right? How is the new black fence *exactly* where the chain link fence was suddenly in your way? And why does this warrant coming over here right this instant, as if it couldn't wait until morning? Have a bad vacation? Do you think the fence is going to walk away tonight on your say-so?" Allie seethed, wanting to smack him, yet still the trees said nothing. She didn't wait for an answer. "I'm not in the mood for this nonsense. Get the hell off my porch *right* now! Your second shall hear from mine."

"You think this is funny? My *lawyer* will be in touch. Let's see you laugh that off!" Bale stepped closer, tilting his chin with his last sentence, practically barking up at Allie who, in her bare feet, was significantly taller. Christopher moved forward simultaneously, Titian and Juniper right behind him.

"Enough!!!" Everyone instantly responded to the command. No motion. No noise. Dorothy Carver, in her voice-of-reason olive sweater set, walked over to Bale and said, "Dorothy Carver, of Stevens, Schmidt & Carver." She coolly pulled a flat golden case from her chinos pocket and extended her business card. Bale looked at it as if confused, then looked back at Dorothy. "Have your attorney contact my assistant at your earliest convenience, thank you. Now, kindly remove yourself from the premises, as my client asked."

Mitchell Bale spun around and clomped down the stairs and short walkway. Before closing the gate from the outside he shouted back, "This isn't over!" as if that were new information. When he had disappeared, the group receded into the house, remembering to be tired again now that the adrenaline rush had subsided.

"I'm really sorry," Allie said softly when they were all slumped into or balled up on the living room couches. She could never do anything right with people. She considered social skills a gift.

"I'm sorry we didn't let you kick his ass!" Dorothy said. She kicked off her shoes. "But as an officer of the court, I thought it best not to spend the night fertilizing your lawn with his remains."

"Right?" Juniper laughed. "What a jackass. All these witnesses in here, we could have claimed it was a home invasion. 'Oh, lordy, we was powerful scared, officers. Allie saved us from the maniac!'" They were all laughing now, half-giddy from the weekend's work and attendant hunger, half relieved that the hostile was gone.

Allie was semi-curled against Christopher, one bare foot on the cream denim couch, her other size-eleven foot on the floor. "I'm glad that's over. Thanks, Dorothy. Nana Nina always said, 'No matter how careful you are with doors opening and closing, no matter how many screens you have, there's always one fly landing on your fresh-baked pie!'"

34

8 The Sound of Her Own Wheels

Allie got out of bed early on Labor Day Monday. There was nothing to do about the neighbor conflict until Dorothy called. It could be days or a week before then. Allie did not feel like sitting home. She was too sad about not having a dog to sit in the quiet house while her friends were at work. One main point of the property-enclosing fence had been to contain a dog. Nana Nina had always had dogs, big red ones named Socrates and Plato. Every time a dog died, a puppy would inherit its name. That's how playful and practical Nana had been. Allie had begun the day by walking to the deserted playground and baseball diamond to lay out a yoga mat and do her exercises with the music from an arm radio. The *Purple Rain* soundtrack cheered her up a bit. Then she hopped the bus to Needham to sit at the Diva Café sketching tunics.

The sense of dread that she would be driven out of her neighborhood by that rude bastard next door was beginning to fade. New jeans and satiny pajamas had made Allie feel sexy, so she had boldly shoved into the master suite, tearing open boxes. She took a huge breath and opened the door to the walk-in closet, afraid to confirm earlier findings. Maybe they were still there, just as everything in the common rooms had been, under and behind objects being prepared for disposal.

All of her shoes were on the left of the closet, blazers and suits on the right. Footwear and jewelry still fit. She would design a wardrobe around them and take all the business skirts and chinos to Goodwill. Allie had worn enough boring clothes to last a lifetime. With tunics and crisp white blouses, she could feel comfortable and attractive again without breaking the bank. It would be nice to get dressed mornings, like people who had real lives, instead of dragging on sweats. There is no dress code for crazy, she kidded around with herself, happy that she could laugh about it. She felt totally free, having left the house without anything covering her, wearing un-bound, medium-length twists for the first time since she had stopped straightening her hair.

Allie took a huge, scared-to-be-hopeful breath and shoved aside the mountain of bags and boxes straight ahead. Then she let out a small peep of relief before sinking to the floor, arms wrapped around her knees. They were still there, from Abba to ZZ Top! Thousands of vinyl records. Her pride, joy, and happiness. She had spent weeks talking herself out of being crushed by their absence...but they were all there.   Here. Allie slid the Eagles from the shelf, plugged in her huge 1950s turntable, and jacked up the volume.

Other than walking past an empty lot with the words "Purgatory Brook" posted on a green and white sign, nothing negative or odd or disturbing had happened that day. Allie had not *done* anything by dusk other than exactly what she pleased. She had drawn pretty pictures, daydreamed, stretched her limbs and limitations, and the world had continued to spin. For so long, Allie had felt the need to keep moving, bustling, hustling, as if inactivity of any sort would have proven her lazy and undeserving of leisure or pleasure. When she got home, she wrote across the top of the refrigerator list of things she had not done. It was an old saying of Nana's: "Tomorrow Ain't Going Nowhere!"

~

Happy to be home for the holidays, Allie lay on her stomach watching television, ankles exed in the air as her pedicure polish dried. Her back reminded: *you overdid that painting thing, wouldn't you say?* From under a CVS hot pack, Allie was completely content even while experiencing a disconnected alien vibe. How curious that four years of TV had passed her by. She was marathon-watching *Breaking Amish*, a show she had not heard of before today. What was today, by the way, and what difference did it make to an unemployed single person? She had no appointments or deadlines.

The feeling was not specifically unpleasant so much as peculiar and untethering. She could float away and the world wouldn't notice. But the midnight blue velvet slipcovers would never be embroidered with silk-stitched cream flowers and fitted onto the living room chairs. Nana's now-cream-denim sofa and loveseat might miss the promised navy piping and sit sulking before the fireplace and freshly-painted cream brick wall. The living room would not meet the sage pillbox pillows that belonged to it. And what other person would realize that the latent merlot stain on the sage, cream, and navy rug had to be treated again to prevent the liquid from climbing the tufts, seeping its way to the top? It might be strange to live for a house, but for now it was at least one reason for Allie to keep going until she balanced and eased into her new world.

Allie could not leave her home. She would fight that bastard who

36

was trying to evil-eye, housing code recite, and otherwise harass her into oblivion. She admired the Amish kids for trying to find new purposes for their lives. That is what Allie was doing too; she realized this while staring at the blank wall until two framed kimonos appeared in her mind's eye, one on each side of the fireplace, with the wall-sconced lights that stayed on overnight aimed at them. She would ask Gabe Junior about raising the lights higher.

Nana Nina's and Marie's kimonos would become art. Just like many items in the house, tacked together new and old, familiar and foreign, given or bought, Allie was being repurposed, redesigning her entire life. Then an idea popped into her head that was so obvious she chuckled in disbelief. Forced to find out about building permits, housing licenses, et cetera, because of her feud-filled, hateful neighbor and his constant official complaints, Allie realized that one can do practically anything she pleases in this life with the proper paperwork. Maybe she could be certified as a yoga instructor! She led three amateur yogis every week. Why not teach five formal students twice per week?

9 Loose Threads

"Do you know a good grass seed I can put down?" Allie asked Dorothy.

"Seed? That's cute, Girlfriend," Dorothy answered. "Sod." It was getting a bit nippy for sitting outside, but they sat on the porch bundled in fleece jackets drinking margaritas anyhow.

"Sod? Like Astroturf?" Allie asked. "The stuff they roll out on HGTV?" She did not want to be rude, but she didn't want a bright-green fake lawn either. She envisioned sitting on the outdoor version of her bedroom window seat, the black wrought-iron half shell of a bench that had been placed over her stump in the back yard. She could almost feel rich soil beneath her toes. The two friends had just hauled loads of trash to the curb and were winding down on Dorothy's last vacation day. Gabe Jr had returned to work the day after the Carvers had come home from Bermuda.

"It's not like that mess from the '70s," Dorothy assured. "It's a tidier, quicker installation of the real thing. Unless you like watching grass grow," she chuckled out. "You like my yard, right."

"Yes! It's beautiful." Allie was cheered even while digesting the thought that she was not like normal adults. In some ways Allie held the past in her mind, and her tableau of what was had not factored in updates or new information. She watched the professionals on her favorite cable channel, but she had not connected the dots to see that many of her beliefs were outdated and she did not have to do everything the hard way to be budget wise and deserving of comfort or small luxuries. Yet, she left many impulse buys stacked unopened until her friends could help her decide what she wanted or needed. At last the number of returns were diminishing as Allie continually practiced impulse control and ordered fewer novelties.

"We can call for an estimate if you like," Dorothy offered, smiling at her beautifully naïve, damaged friend, the closest she had ever come to a sister, neither she nor Gabe Junior having a blood sister.

"You think I can lay it down myself?" Allie asked in an excited tone.

"I know you could. But Gabe and Tre will do it. They knocked ours out in one Saturday swoop with Bobby Lee and Levi."

"Gabe's brother, Bobby Lee?" Allie sounded pleased at her knowledge.

"That's right. Levi too. Have you met them?" Dorothy prompted.

"Just Bobby Lee. And the other brother Elvis was in my home-room. We went out once," Allie said, disappointed that she had forgot an entire human. A fourth brother? There were four?

"Ellll-vis!" Dorothy laughed out. "Oh, Lordy, that's hilarious! "Elvis" is Levi's real name. Nobody but his mama still calls him that!"

Allie laughed too. "Oh, that IS funny! I don't blame him. You couldn't PAY me to answer to the Nuclears' tag, 'Mary Allison'!"

"They. Did. *Not*! You're kidding me. What kinda folks name a little Black girl like that?!" Dorothy questioned, laughing even harder.

"Blonde wannabees, that's what stripe!" Allie guffawed.

"I can't believe you two dated," Dorothy said. "I have to interact with him because we're family. He's good looking, but the polar opposite of my Gabe, personality wise. I wasn't exactly amazed when his wife ran off with that electrician. Should've seen my phony *Naw, really?* face! I was thinking, 'Run for it, sister. Zoom!'"

"Soooo funny," Allie agreed. "He was just *too too* pompous on our first slash last date! It is *seriously* hard to believe they are blood brothers. Wow, I missed a lot of the juicy gossip."

"No worries, Sister Allie...plenty more where that came from! Hey, what is all this stuff on your porch? Close-out sale at Modes?" Dorothy had just noticed that Allie's modest haul was incoming.

"It *is* fabric. And some notions. Want to see? Coffee first? It's for reupholstering though. I went to Lucy's in Davis Square and got two chests for my sewing room. This is for the slipper chair," Allie excitedly jumbled out all her carefully planned creative thoughts.

"Coffee is a great idea!" Dorothy said, nodding her head. They went in to put on a pot of Deathwish, dragging parcels indoors and shutting out the brisk evening.

10 Allie – Oops!

Allie was acting calm, but it was just a ruse; she was planning to make a run for it the instant the nurse was out of sight. It was still difficult to fathom. She had been raking leaves. Cherry-red leaves from her big, luscious tree miscegenated with just-fallen, newly curling, squat golden maples from the highway neighbor's yard and totally furled, skinny, dry mustard oaks from the asshole neighbor's driveway. Allie had been frightened for a moment when Mitchell Bale had appeared in front of her. She must be hallucinating! Oh, God, had she forgotten her medicine? She did not think so, but even while replaying the mental image of her left hand reaching past an egg-white omelet with salsa verde and turkey sausage toward the medicine bottle on the bare wood table of the kitchen nook, Allie thought she must be mistaken. But then, unbelievably, Bale threw something at her. She had ducked but in a swoosh of instinct had also backhanded Bale with the rake. There was screaming, the whining shriek of an ambulance, police – all kinds of hell breaking loose – yet it was a curiously-muffled complaining world that Allie had heard. Apparently, she had fallen and banged her head.

The nurse disappeared, so Allie lurched from the emergency room's crib of a bed and hurried toward the door, such as it was, elated that they had neither cuffed nor tied her down. She could not understand why she was free, but all that truly concerned her at the moment was remaining that way. And who wanted to go back in time, to listen to the long-winded assessment of all that was wrong in her ramshackled excuse for a mind? She had taken good care of herself for months, and she had never been violent in life, despite her problems. It was so unfair that one reprehensible excuse for a human could just stroll into her neighborhood, come tromping through her life, even storm into her freakin' yard, and undo all her hard work to patch her mind and home back together. The other shoe had finally dropped.

Bam! Allie cleared the curtain of the small sick bay, but her victory was short-lived as she fell, hard, onto her right shoulder. The nurse came hurrying back, along with a male nurse and Christopher, who must have been called as the second emergency contact, Juniper being in Vermont for the week.

"Oh, honey! Where are you going?" The nurse asked. *Angie.* Her nametag said so. She and the other nurse helped Allie back to bed. Allie began to cry.

"I didn't do anything," Allie explained, in the hurt voice of a falsely-accused child. "He came in my yard. I was raking leaves."

"Of course, Allie Oops," Christopher said, sounding extremely concerned even while trying to calm Allie down. "Nobody thinks you did one. Wrong. Thing. That blithering idiot was treated and arrested an hour ago."

"He's not dead?" Allie brightened some, even while seeking confirmation before gratefully sinking into the cold pack that Nurse Angie was deftly arranging on the pillow with one hand while pulling a white thermal blanket over Allie with the other.

"Dead? Lord, no, Sistah. With all the booze he was snookered up on? He barely felt it. His arm isn't even broken. It will just be really sore when his pickle juice wears off. And there was a whole yard full of teenagers next door playing football. Saw the whole scene. They came over the fence to grab him after you went down."

"It was like light speed. I'm raking. Crazy jerk is in my yard. Something's flying at me as he's charging. I swing at the asshole." Allie was incredulous now that she was calming down from the lack of a murder charge. The nurse was fussing over her, handing her ginger ale with a bendy straw. The bendy straw made Allie feel safe. "Thank you." She smiled at Nurse Angie.

"You're welcome," Nurse Angie said, "now you stay put okay? You were unconscious for an hour and need to rest until you're more steady on your feet."

"Okay. How come I was unconscious?" Allie thought she had fainted from anxiety.

Christopher and the nurse looked at each other as if deciding who should speak. But the doctor stepped into the bay just then, so he answered while shaking Allie's hand, "Hello, Ms. Kenyon. I'm Dr. Bradford. You had quite a bump on your head from a package that was thrown at you. Excellent reflexes! It caught you on the side of your head, enough to throw you off balance as you swung...a rake, was it?" His head bent to read off of the clipboard.

"Yes. I was raking leaves. They were so pretty," Allie reminisced out loud about her favorite season. "What package?" Christopher fielded the question as Nurse Angie excused herself from the small space. "That charmer accepted your mis-delivered UPS box then used it as an excuse to go into your yard to pick a fight."

"Oh! I was off in my own world and didn't even notice him until

41

he was running at me, yelling something. By the time I saw some-thing flying at me, it was too late. I had no idea what it was. It must have been Socrates's bed," Allie explained, excited that everything was falling into place, making sense, and that nobody thought her a dangerous, institution-worthy psycho. Dumbass had started it.

"Socrates?" Dr. Bradford asked while checking under the ice pack on the left side of Allie's head.

"I just got a dog. He's red," Allie said proudly. The dog was the last piece of the normalizing of Nana Nina's home. One wall had been whacked down. A dog had been added. That symbolized a balance to Allie. *Respect the past, but accept change* was the sentence Allie had re-stenciled in a black wave of words on the wall over the built-in 1960s kitchen nook. "His nickname is 'Old Sock'," Allie continued, enjoying Nana's old joke.

"Good one!" Dr. Bradford chuckled.

~

A month later it was snowing and Christopher, who had moved into the guest room for a week to be around for Allie, had been forsaken by his husband-in-name-only. Then Allie had invited him to stay until he found a man who deserved him.

"I could be here forever!" Christopher joked.

"Fine by me," Allie had said, and she meant it. She was surprised to enjoy living with another person, but it was nice to have someone else who loved the old house with whom to enjoy it. She went to estate sales and thrift shops with Christopher. His special dish being deviled eggs, he was a willing guinea pig for Allie's experiments in healthier cooking. Christopher also helped with the paperwork that overwhelmed Allie and made her feel frightened that she would make one false move and lose everything all over again.

Dorothy, Juniper, and Christopher had sat down to explain to Allie that she had way more money than she realized. They worked out her schedules and helped her file all appropriate documentation to continue delegating responsibilities to her Nana's long-term employees. Allie's friends helped her to budget and save without living as if she were still on food stamps, living in a pay-by-the-week boardinghouse. Now that she had a licensed yoga studio with ten clients and was selling her clothing and home designs via Nana Nina's Shoppe along with the pies and homemade sundries, Allie had a comfy income and a small empire to run. Learning to trust

42

had not been easy, but it was gradually becoming normal for people to care for her and make her feel necessary to their lives too. The four friends saved one yoga class just for themselves and Titian. Allie ran a second class for six students, four neighborhood mothers and two of their friends. But she still had plenty of time to read in her library and sew for pleasure and stress therapy in her bumblebee seamstress room, finished with Christopher only a week before the violent Mitchell Bale incident.

After all of his flag-planting, bullying harassment based on the encroachment of Allie's fence and trees into his yard, it turned out that technically his driveway was Allie's property. Nana Nina's own hand-drawn blueprints had been in her safety deposit box. Dorothy Carver had sent some of her law students to research the case. Most of Kensington Road's residents had driveways to the right of their houses, but a double-sized driveway had been poured to the right of Bale's house; half of it was legally his, so he had been feuding with the wrong neighbor. Nana Nina's documents clearly delineated the property lines, but she had used a gravel driveway along the front side of the house that was built facing the wrong way. Thus, her back yard on the highway was huge, meant to be the front. And her front yard was small, intended to be the back.

At any rate, good old Bale got out of jail and sold the house that was killing him now that his wife had left him. Then he moved to Rehoboth. He sent Allie a Christmas card, which she marveled over even more than his unloading a house in December. The new neighbors were dull and insular. Perfect!

Allie had always wondered what it would feel like to have a little brother, a man who did not make outrageous demands then make her feel like dirt if she could not possibly meet them. Interactions with her father had felt like hostage negotiations. Every time she got close to ransoming her normal life or even some measure of dignity, good ol' Sterling would raise the price and alter the rules. Then, the men she had slept with expected her to "come around some day." *Come around* translates to: do what I want or be who I assumed you were when we met. Men craved her, but not one lover had ever accepted and loved *her*. But Christopher did. He showed up one day and instantly loved her; she loved him too. They were family now, regardless of how long they lived under the same roof.

A work friend of Allie, Deb, used to joke with her. "Look at you! You're a goddess! You don't just need *a man*. You need a *gay man*...someone who knows how to treat a lady when she's wearing panties.

Christopher was given total creative freedom to re-do the guest suite. Allie had previously decided on cream and deep golden striped walls. The taupe mantle and hearth partnered with lush, ceiling-to-floor, taupe velvet drapes made the room seem to her cozy as well as luxurious and large. Christopher concurred and added a taupe headboard with black linens, gold and cream easy chairs with black pillows, and a taupe area rug over the dark-stained, varnished floorboards. Two huge black and white photo collages hung on the windowed wall. A large urban-industrial black metal clock hung over the mantle. The bathroom was taupe with cream towels and black-framed photos. Allie's prized albums still covered one entire shelved closet wall, exactly where she had left them five years earlier. Christopher used the *His* closet in the master suite for storage as well as wardrobe. His statues, small photos, and other traveling souvenirs filled in spaces on new, floating-glass shelves in the sunny bedroom. But the albums stayed in their cool, dark space.

By December, the roommates spent most common evenings after dinner hanging out in the master suite listening to music, dancing and drinking in front of the fireplace. The living room barely saw them together during the week. It was rare, however, for the old house not to find its weekend living room inhabited by a minimum of six friends enjoying the fire while snow stacked up and up and up.

Part 2: Rosebud

26 tales of 26 very different
New England women

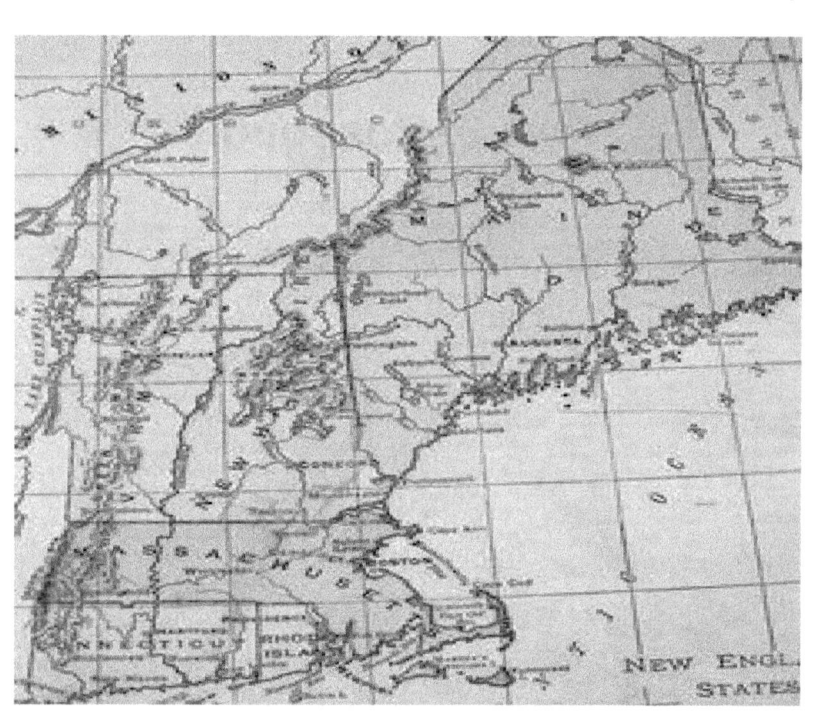

Contents of Rosebud

Contents, continued

Rosebud

~

Bunny Slippers

Gretchen wrote tiny stories. Not just the length of them was abbreviated. There was no distilled emotion – as in the terror of Poe – nor a cultural flavor that instilled a pleasant temporary sense of belonging, as in Sandra Cisneros's tales. Nor did Gretchen have a huge political point to drive home to her readers. No brilliant, subversive artistry shrouded her cause. Gretchen had simply loved stories since she was a little girl propping open large picture books, eyes as wide and vibrant as the watercolors.

Despite her lack of a particular goal, Gretchen loved the tiny tales dearly and would read them to herself on lonely nights to keep from watching *It's a Wonderful Life* in June. Gretchen was a hopeful romantic. Sighing into the snowbound tableau of the last tray table remaining from her Grammie's 1950s kitchen, she'd picture her mother's pond-skating and skiing childhood rather than her own happy but city-locked youth. Her reflections on her own life were rather balanced, some pros and some cons, some rough years polka-dotted with blissful periods or moments. Her loneliness had been sad enough, but not tragic. But the pleasing moments were not quaint enough to fill a New England snow globe or a Rockwell-worthy painting.

Gretchen earned a living illustrating children's books and greeting cards, sepia with photo album corners drawn or painted in. A certain fabricated melancholia helped pay the mortgage on her great room with fireplace and ladder-to-loft cottage on the South Shore of Massachusetts. Gretchen lived an isolated life when she chose and took the commuter rail to South Station in Boston each Saturday for a pancake breakfast. Her college friend Betty Green-Lined in from Newton. Diana came in from Charles Street. An occasional fourth showed up in the revolving seat, but the trio of friends were steadfast.

Every now and again Betty's husband fixed Gretchen up with an eligible bachelor. Diana rolled her asexual eyes, sighing heavily through the description of Mr. Right. Polite dinner dates ensued, but Gretchen was relieved, elated even, when safely ensconced in the high-backed, wine vinyl cushion of the commuter train car, putt-putt-

3

ing home with a good book. She liked sex…a lot. None of the fairly nice but dull dates tossed off enough testosterone for Gretchen to consider a lifestyle change.

Back home, Gretchen would light a fire, pour a glass of Frey Merlot, and sit, blissful in bunny slippers, snuggled in her Eddie Bauer pajamas. Sometimes she watched Lifetime movies while reading. Often, Gretchen just enjoyed the fiery light and warmth. Then she sat up to write a story, exactly five paragraphs long, before falling asleep.

Today I Pretend to Be Denise

In the fourth grade, back in Roxbury where I'm from, there was a party. The Wise potato chips were very good, not greasy or green-edged like some times. And I never care to this day what-all is served at a party as long as the chips are good. Chips and root beer. Chips and organic wine. No difference. A good chip makes any party bearable.

None of it makes a difference to you, maybe. And I'm sorry for that. But I have a need to say that I was never, ever a connected girl. Unpopularity is not the point here. The complete, abject, floating sense of disconnection must be communicated. That's the crux of the story, the axle that makes it roll to its natural conclusion.

On that afternoon – for they always had day's-end parties in elementary school, getting everyone all hopped up on cake with gritty blue and yellow pastel frosting and orange Fanta before sending us home to mothers who'd spent the entire morning sloshing laundry and sweeping – then there was a special feeling in the air, almost a scent. Spring had everyone going, even the teachers.

On this day when something was bound to happen, a boy's birthday cake had pink and yellow frosting. Nobody laughed though. It was that type of congeniality and joy of living and laughing circulating in the classroom. Forty-five years ago. But I remember what happened next, how everyone was transfixed by her. Stevie Wonder's sound began. And when it did, "Sir Duke" magically took over Denise's body and all of our spirits.

So today, when the sky is black with rain for a sixth day in June, I put it on. Stevie. The fourth grade. Elementary joy. And I'm not alone. Or poor. And my socks are not grey because I'm allergic to bleach and my mother, who died three years ago, cannot remind me of the vinegar whitening recipe for the umpteenth time. For today, I pretend I am Denise. A serpentine shimmy esses through my usually stiff body. Neck to heels, I turn liquid. Arms undulate, long, longer, longest.   Knees disappear.   My hips are a swinging pendulum.   My booty goes all Alvin Ailey, wading aqua silk waters under golden cherubs at the Wang Centre.

Miriam Made No Promises

Miriam made no promises, especially to herself. There was, therefore, no reason she could fathom to turn down a set-up coffee date the same day that she had a dinner date of her own devising. It is often assumed that a 50-year-old woman whose children have been booted from the nest can't find a substantial husband to replace the one she has willfully ejected from her bed. Raising two great foster kids rather than a half-grown mate seemed a better use of Miriam's time. But she loved sex.

So here Miriam was, sitting at one of the last Mug 'n' Muffins left in Massachusetts waiting quaintly for her *he's already-late-would-it-be-rude-of-me-to-order-a-muffin* blind date. Her dear friends were two of the teachers on her staff, History and Math. They never asked the middle-aged principal about her love life, just assuming it was nonexistent. Well, Miriam was a touch old-fashioned, but she was no prude.

Just as the daydream of square sugar crystals on a blueberry muffin top was beginning to frazzle Miriam's nerves, Mr. Unknown showed up with a "Hiya!" Great. Dating *Rhoda*. Miriam had wanted to *be* television's Rhoda back in the years of longing to move to New York to become a designer then write for a fashion magazine. Now she looked and sounded more like a Black Mary Tyler Moore. Relaxed bob. Ralph Lauren scarf instead of her usual pearls. Navy pants and Talbot's flats with gold pilgrim buckles.

Friends' taste in men had improved over the years. Or maybe the pool was larger from all of the recent divorces. He was goofy and nervous but also approximately 6'4" and cute as his buttoned-down blue and white striped shirt. Well, okay, she would forgive his dark chest hair for a mere eleven minutes of tardiness. She was almost shocked though. Her White friends had set her up with a White man. That never would have happened twenty years ago. They hadn't even mentioned race at all.

The times sure are a-changin' she thought. It was 8:30 p.m. and Miriam was attempting to concentrate on the man who was buying her scallops and urging her to take "just a bitty sip" of white wine.

7

She hated white wine and had already explained that it gave her migraines. Jerk. Another wasted Saturday night. But there would be Sundays, Mondays, Tuesdays, perhaps weeks of "well, maybe this time" muffins.

Whereabouts

Pasha had done her share of walking. She always had a driver now. Her husband was bemused by her. Three personal shoppers picked and shipped clothes appropriate for Pasha's public appearances as Christopher's wife. Otherwise, she dressed for comfort. She was grateful for jewelry yet not enthralled by it. A $12.00 table red tasted fine to her. The simplest life possible in the cul-de-sac of an historic home in Brookline. Yet Pasha would not walk farther than the CVS in Coolidge Corner and had not been on the *T* since before her wedding. After her long bachelor-woman life of being exposed to Boston weather while waiting for trains and buses, walking when she was too broke to ride – which was often – having a driver made Pasha feel safe and free.

Because the sun made Pasha itchy and dizzy, in warmer months she covered up like a beekeeper with a scarf tied over a large straw hat. Both that look and her disdain for pedestrian activity had earned Patricia Jane the nickname "Pasha" from her girlfriends. After twenty-five years of friendship, she accepted their teasing as love and even began introducing herself as Pasha. Her honey-tan skin and habits of wearing knee-grazing tunics, lengthy scarves, cat-framed sunglasses and carrying a small gold wristlet bag caused a lack of questioning about her unusual moniker. She was eccentric, conspicuous. Her name fit.

But this was an early-November evening and there was a flat tire. It was quite cold outside without the hostile glare of the sun. Pasha read in the warm car as the minor inconvenience was followed by a flat spare, was followed by her shrieking at the driver, was followed by his stomping off. Abandoned, Pasha went from triumphant – for finally chastising the driver's consistent negligence of the vehicle – to petrified in record time. She sat down in the back seat, ballerina flats on the concrete of an unfamiliar sidewalk, and waited to be rescued. But no one came.

Where was she? Why hadn't she paid attention? If her freedom depended on recalling where she'd been after leaving the Chestnut Hill Atrium Mall two hours earlier, she'd be tossed in the clink for lack of an alibi. Pasha had bought her husband a shirt and two ties.

9

And for herself, a sumptuous tea rose lipstick. That much she could account for. Then she'd read *Shakespeare Saved My Life* on her Kindle until the *thunk, thunk, thunking* tire drew her attention. Pasha suddenly laughed at herself! This was no mountain or forest, for goodness sake. Pasha pulled out her cell phone.

At Christopher's calm cajoling, Pasha left the car to tentatively inspect her whereabouts. She walked slowly, shivering from stark terror as well as cold. Despite the teal shawl draped over her head and double-neck-wrapped, she felt naked outside without sunglasses. The sign under the streetlamp read "Tappan St." Pasha used to live off of Corey Road and walk to the Star Market on the corner of Beacon Street and Tappan. Encouraged, Pasha marched to Beacon to wait for the C Line home. An irate Christopher fired the livery service. Pasha occasionally took cabs.

Better Than Fiction

Rebecca had truly believed that she and her new roommates would form a cluster of best girlfriends. Like those of a murdered go-go dancer who were interviewed by 1970s television detectives: "You'll catch them, won't you? She was like a sister to me." Or, both divorced and over 60, she and her instant best friends would eat cheesecake in kimonos at 2 a.m. whenever one of them was all broken-up over some guy.

Divorce couldn't kill Rebecca's belief in true love – or unrequited love – or even the value of really effed up *why-are-boys-so-dumb*? love. She still taught *Wuthering Heights* and *Jane Eyre* in her introductory literature courses. Rebecca's marriage had been lonely for more than ten years. Truth be told, her girlfriends of the past twenty years had been circumstantial, so her husband got them in the divorce. Rebecca had "won" the house, sold it, bought a two-bedroom condo smack in the heart of Providence, Rhode Island.

The cheap rent and furnished room had lured Loretta (65 and totally financially screwed by her lawyer husband's lawyer). A part-time office manager at Brown, Loretta had cheated, yet she complained of being mistreated after being left by her lover too. Her sense of entitlement and embittered fury was juicy business to docile, long-suffering Rebecca. Rebecca had never loved or loathed sex. It was just there, much like cooking. She was quite competent at both, but didn't have a passion for either despite compliments on her abilities.

Loretta the temptress did not care for humans as a species. They were all incompetent actors or undeserving audiences in her very scripted, melodramatic life. Rebecca did try to keep up. But she could not always clap loud and long enough for Loretta. Ultimately, Rebecca turned to evenings spent with red wine and reading Poe's short stories for her book club. Loretta smoked on the porch, screaming and crying into her cell at her latest swain after swain after swain. Then she packed and flapped off in an unannounced flutter, leaving a filthy room in her wake and pilfering Rebecca's grandmother's pearls.

Then Doris moved in, introducing her friend Patty to the domestic dynamic. Rebecca took a lover, Andrew, who became a boyfriend, and she made new friends on the commuter rail. They were all very dull but liked wine and potluck movie nights at Patty's house in Hyde Park. So five women would now be part of Rebecca's golden years. They nicknamed her "Beck". Andrew never met any of Beck's friends. He was always busy perfecting some new recipe for his five-star restaurant.

Rosebud

Augusta set out maple cream sandwich cookies and chocolate-dipped, almond tea biscuits. Every Sunday at 4 p.m. the girls came over. It was a lovely tradition, and she enjoyed catching up on her friends' lives. But mostly, Augusta was the life of the party and she relished it. All the girls were riveted, anticipating when the conversation turned to sex.

"Lusty Gusty" shone through stories all beginning with the same three magic words, "That reminds me...." Augusta had overcome a strict, traditionalist upbringing, thoroughly enjoying the male species throughout grad school, and her thirties...and her forties.... At 55, she was taking a break to write a book *Southern Ladies of New England: A Guide*. The consummate, genteel hostess on paper, she was a pistol in person, much like her ancestral foremothers.

In her thirty-five year reign of terror over every clueless, love-besotted sap who innocently strolled into her sights, Augusta had spent just enough time with each man to generate public use of the word "serious." Then, her blood ran cold and she walked out of his life. She was not cruel. She simply could not bear another creature breathing in her gold and crème dream house, watching sports and calling her "honey." And what would she do with him at tea time?

So Augusta entertained the frustrated, the extramarital adventuring, the secretly coupled, the lifelong celibate, and the happily legally conjoined Southern-style ladies of Massachusetts. She wondered how she'd ended up there. Augusta had grown up with five brothers, playing with Hot Wheels cars, G.I. Joes, pipe cleaner men, and action figures. She could debate the merits of Barry Smith's *Conan the Barbarian* illustrations versus John Buscema's. Her dirt patties held together better than any boy's. And nobody wanted to mess with her marble-shooting thumbs. It had been marvelous and had made her brave and direct and full of self-confidence. Then followed one professional success after another. Everything she touched thrived, especially the small patch of garden on her grounds that she attended herself.

But for five decades "Lusty Gusty" had longed for the tea parties of her youth, with Daddy and rag dolls. One day she sent out invitations for a high tea fundraiser. Total strangers showed up for what was now known as the party of the year. But for fifty-one weeks a year, Augusta got what she really wanted. Friends who came for Sunday tea when there were no flashbulbs or reporters or millionaires. The bell rang as Gusty put the last fresh rosebud in an individual vase at the dining table. She stopped only to check her smiling face in the gold-framed mirror in the entryway. Then she opened the heavy glass and iron-scrolled door to welcome her life.

Not Getting a Break

Clove was a baker who was bored with jokes about "spicing up" dessert, et cetera. Why do people expect a person to be amused by jokes made at her expense? Unlike most other professional chefs and bakers she had met, Clove disliked rooms full of people – adoring, wise-cracking, or otherwise. Confident in how good her work was, she did not need compliments. But she flared up at the slightest critique. Her work had become her entire life, and she took commentary on it as a personal insult or intrusion. Clove rationalized that she *would* socialize if she weren't surrounded by morons.

Clove was drinking her third Christmas beer while dusting 500 raspberry Linzer stars with confectioner's sugar. Who in hell needs 500 cookies at an adult party? Give her a plate of cold cuts and a fine ale any day! The beer was horrible. She had a whole case, given by a slobbering fan. No, truly. He was sloshing drunk, with barbeque sauce polka-dotting his Santa tie. Security had escorted him from the set, but in a rare moment of compassion Clove had thanked the man face to face and ordered that he be driven home. It had been Christmas eve, after all, and the large studio audience could boost her career considerably.

Ah, Clove thought, *cold cuts*. She rummaged through the refrigerator and found a good salami and a leftover slab of maple bacon. Now that the swill was made nectar, Clove's mania kicked in. Ha! To hell with catering. Of course the My Compliments! network would pick up her series, market her book.... Clove wrapped the cookies in green cellophane and red mesh then tied and curlicued thin gold ribbon to cinch out any air. She fell asleep for hours but shook herself awake after the second cartoon dream ghost appeared with foolish admonishments. Dickens indeed!

That evening Clove carried the cookies from Arlington Street to Charles Street rather than wait around for the *T* or a cab on Christmas Day. In the park children were making a snowman; a pair of lovers strolled by the snow-filled swan lagoon as if it were spring. The old green suspension bridge almost got the better of her and her delicate creations. Why had she crossed it in such breezy

15

weather? Feeling oddly light, she ran to the Boston Common side, almost fluttering to the corner. A woman in a motorized scooter, also waiting to cross Beacon Street, smiled up at Clove from under a yellow, cabled hat. Unsure why, Clove beamed back as the two crossed. *Zoom!* A car blew through the red light. Clove automatically lunged out to swerve the woman out of harm's way. Assured repeatedly that the uncommonly calm woman was okay, Clove retrieved her cookies and sat shaking over a gingerbread latté at Starbucks. Sadly, she opened the package to inspect the remnants of her long night of work.

A gasp surprised Clove. It was her own, as she looked at the perfect confections. Not one break. Clove finished her coffee and skipped down the street to make her delivery. The customer was very pleased, then dismayed to discover that Clove had no plans for Christmas. While being invited to stay for the party, Clove could still hear the yellow-hatted woman saying, "You were very brave. You are a good person. Always remember." Clove removed her hat, looked in the hall mirror at her stunning face, patted her silver hair…and did remember. She had always been a good person, but it had been a very long time since anyone had noticed the human behind the masterpiece.

Viola

Masters Class 128 was overpriced and bursting with inflated egos and libidos. Viola, who had played the oboe in the *Nutcracker Suite* for twenty seasons, was hungover. Nobody noticed even when she blatantly pulled a monogrammed silver flask from her black velvet blazer pocket and took a swig. Row 15 in the Coolidge Corner Theatre was full of non-actors who were bored in their own arts and trying to get laid via a Meetup.com event. Like Viola.

Damn, it was only Thanksgiving. In the old days elders betrothed kids before they were born. Later, there were barn dances or Jack and Jill parties, depending on one's socioeconomic and ethnic circumstances. In the '80s, friends invited the divorced or abandoned to parties in secret pairs, hoping they might find each other. Nowadays, however, Viola bitterly noted, normal single women were screwed. Fending for themselves against hoards of gym-going, calorie-counting, $500 spa-tripping man tacklers. Viola had met, slept with, and disengaged from three Mr. Rightnow men in two years. The men had been sleepwalkers, mechanically moving through relationships. Viola wanted passion at least, if not actual full-blown love.

Well, Viola had just found a date for her BFF anyhow. Joss was gay and always in love with reed-thin, melodramatic bimbos but "dying to settle down and have 'young-uns'." The classmate who had hit on Viola was smart, funny, and had a real job. A bottle-strawberry-blonde physical therapist with huge bazookas. Joss loved bazookas. Viola was mentally picking out her maid of honor dress at Nordstrom's in Chestnut Hill when someone asked for a sip. Startled, Viola slithered her hand into the stranger's denim jacket and released the flask.

He winked down at her. Hadn't shaved. Looked like Starsky, for chrissake. Hot damn! And then they were fake cops and robbers in the class exercise for an intensive hour. Then Viola flipped Warren and her flask tumbled from his faded Old Navy classic onto the worn wooden planks of the stage. They both ran. "Up from the floor there arose such a clatter," they chanted while walking and laughing down Harvard toward Warren's apartment on Brighton Ave.

By New Year's Eve the lovers were inseparable. And even Viola's father loved Warren, not Jewish and jewelry artist though he may be. He had a day job and a condo in the go-green luxury complex. He hammered the ring band for Viola himself. They both quit acting classes. After all, they had finally found their motivation. And a couple can be engaged forever.

Strings

Sweet, energizing Vivaldi perfumed the air. Spring, musically. But it was summer in Wanda's trailer and she was entirely too undereducated, untrained, unspoiled, to know or care better. Sometimes details just mess up pleasure. Blissful Wanda soared high on spring wings.

Clip. *Bam!* Oh, Lord's sake, what was it that had spoiled her joy? *Bam! Bam! Bam!* As if all human life depended on the knocker's satisfaction. Wanda flung open the door, ready to voice her how-Earthly-necessary-is-this? query. Claudia stood, dripping wet with eyes swollen. It wasn't raining.

"Girl?" Wanda's voice heightened in concern and surprise, anger evaporating. Claudia fell up the stairs as Wanda slam-locked the door, no questions asked, reaching for her gun. Last thing she'd shot was a rabid raccoon back in her Grandpappy's attic one year, the terror-filled elders clinging together in the den. One shot. Kerplunk!

Bam! He was in. *Bang!* He was down. End of drama. Without interlude. Wanda had had her own share of man drama in her life. Plugging a lunatic was just one of many rapid routes to one of many possible endings. But Claudia started screaming, and, well, screaming in a trailer park gets crap going. Wanda shook her friend. Hard. Claudia stunned up, puckered her lips, stood with beating-puffed eyes and a confused treble on her mouth. Wanda softened her "case closed" face and motioned a *shush* until Claudia nodded.

They drove down Route 1A North days later, sweet rolls in the kitchenette and delicious Vivaldi on the iPod dock. Wanda had no idea who found Mick's body. When? Who knew what? And who was hot on her trail, if anyone? Wanda was 75 and her best friend was 30. They had music, gas money, food, and the belief that true love was waiting once again at the next rest stop.

Love Is

At 3am she was subconsciously violating the first rule of some schools of writers: Don't write about writing. But Bennie had been out of school for a very long time and had no use for draconian rule makers who had zero self-discipline despite two divorces and twenty years of therapy, not to mention grown children who wouldn't mention them around normal-parented friends. Sometimes Bennie was offended to be lumped in with the immature, narcissistic stereotypes. Other times, she pitied their insecurity. Most people she knew who were 45ish to 60ish had come from broken homes of one sort or another. Her parents had been hardasses, but they had toughed it out together and set up rules.

Heart-wracking sobs woke Bennie up, which was a shame since she'd been dreaming of the Red Sox seventh-inning stretch tribute. Elton John serenaded her while Ben Affleck handed her a plaque in recognition of her contribution to something unspecific but definitely related to writing. Great. The perfect dream — watching herself read the perfect plaque — interrupted by a whiner. Jolted by the reality of her only actual bed mate of ten years, Bennie sat up. She reached a circle of arms around her husband automatically. He sobbed himself back to sleep, snuggling her tan breasts with his wet, red-flushed face.

While Sheldon cooked eggs at 10am Bennie was mentally writing a poem about his eyes, but lingering behind the romance was what might cause a grown, stereotypically macho man to bawl in his sleep after going to bed in his usual efficient fashion: lights off *Click!* head hits pillow *Zzzz.* Right after the news. And Sheldon apparently had no idea his middle-of-night crying jag had happened.

Bennie closed her eyes and saw Sheldon in the black granite, burgundy, and forest green kitchen whistling while he whisked. He loved to cook and loved Bennie's butt no matter what size it was. Sheldon was Bennie's living fantasy, with a shaggy-headed John Schneider silhouette and singing CCR tunes at the top of his gruff and gritty lungs, punctuating seasoning with an Emeril *Bam!* as drum beat. *It ain't me, Lord. It ain't me... Bam! Bam! Bam!* At work he was all JR, ruthless in a suit and textured cowboy boots.

Bennie felt guilty that Sheldon's family had ostracized him. A good ol' boy with a Black woman? And he hadn't just worked out an itch and then re-found his senses, he'd married her. The only Black woman south of the Mason-Dixon who couldn't cook for beans or recognize a real job...even before. A Northern, uselessly educated, uppity African-American wife? Saints preserve! Her parents had tried to take her back. Why hadn't he just let them? Bennie wondered if they had a family outside themselves, would someone please help her understand why her sweet husband was so upset? Sheldon sat down, kissing Bennie's head en route to his chair. "Plate of toast at 3:00," he guided her, placing a fork in her hand.

Too Few To Mention

Sonia suddenly realized while watching, of all things, an archaeology adventure flick starring Matthew McConaughey, that home meant a sewing machine. It was what she needed after all these years of catching up to even the palest fleeting shadows of childhood dreams, doing everything to some extent to keep from ever having one of those "Oh, I wish I had done _____" lives. To feel settled at last, to live in one place long enough to buy furniture, and to make a nice pair of pants and a tunic.

Truthfully, Sonia was looking for a hobby to replace dating. She hadn't run out of prospects so much as run low on energy for the too-young or interest in the age-appropriate but embittered. She had a few more sips of Finn. Merlot then virtually pointed and clicked to order a Singer. The smallest decision or commitment required a huge emotional self-nudge for her; thus, the liquid courage.

Realizing that her well-ordered and organized life had only veered toward all or nothing in one area before, love, at 59 Sonia was becoming an all-around extremist. Jump from a plane without a 'chute, freefall into love, make beautiful things or buy average instead. Or don't bother. Satisfying lust was another matter; she saw the difference and was guiltless regarding sex minus love. When hungry, eat. It's part of being human. Sonia used the rest of night to cut out patterns, stacking future outfits on the folding table she kept under the bed. She drank and cut, ignored the phone, and drank and cut. Exhausted by sun-up, she crawled into bed happy and tipsy.

Michael's in the Porter Square mall beckoned to Sonia's creative-binging mind. She pushed a cart laden with bric-a-brac, flower- and heart-shaped buttons, and lady-bug bias tape into line. Raising her eyes to return the smile of the man ahead of her in line, who refused a bag and carried two cans of spray paint in one hand, Sonia fixated on his top button even after he had left. Then she moved slowly through a daydream. She saw herself mutely frowning at him, confused about her role in the scene.

Then she realized that the daydreamt Sonia could not remember how to tie a man's tie. Once, it had been just part of her morning routine. Make coffee; cook eggs; toast bagels; watch her incredibly capable grown man frown at his image in the hall mirror as he fumbles, sighs, unties. Move his hands. Tie it for him. Accept his thank-you-and-bye-'til-later combo smooch. Close the door and go about your day. Sonia now sat in her car thinking about her last serious lover's shortcomings. Too few to mention, she thought, reaching for her cell phone to return his call.

Second Worst

Tanya's best friend was the worst capital-*b* Bitch on Mama Earth. This fact was highlighted for everyone who met the pair by the fact that Tanya's noteworthily nasty friend was a man. Ford sent food back to kitchen restaurants a minimum of once per month, pitching an insult-ridden snit the entire time. Once, he had thrown "ill-chilled" champagne in the waiter's face before storming from Copley Place. Tanya had tossed twenties and *I'm-so-sorry's* while following her irate buddy.

On Halloween eve, Tanya and Ford now sat at Hungry Mother near Kendall Square. Tanya hoped Ford wouldn't act up too badly because she loved the upscale soul food restaurant. They had already been banned for life from the converted firehouse restaurant on Main Street. Of course, that was before Tanya had been forced to move out of Woburn and Ford had sold his own condo and bought them a house in Watertown out of guilt. Like many upper-middle-class professionals, they lived in Watertown yet mostly hung out in Cambridge. Ford had been right about the lawn jockeys, but right isn't always legal, especially at 3am.

Tanya sighed out her relief, stretching her long sueded legs into a relaxed ex, and watching Ford's green eyes sparkle by tea light. He was enchanted by the boiled peanuts. When in love with his food, Ford was a dream of a man. He beamed out his dinner order to the lovely, light banter of a waitress. Tanya savored her pecan sauce, pondering the redundancy of pecan pie for dessert. Then the pair walked to the Charles and strolled arm-in-arm along the River before Ford drove home, with Tanya beginning to doze on his shoulder. Ford looked at Tanya's lips, shellacked red beneath the bowler borrowed from his costume.

The next morning Tanya was calling in a favor. Her college friend swooped into the police station and managed to keep Ford from getting booked. Everything had vanished — paperwork...furious complainant...even the cane Ford had used to smash in the windows of the off-centered yellow jeep that had only barely scratched his Porsche when pulling into the driveway at 4am.

By Christmas, Tanya's family was not speaking to her much less tempting demons by inviting Ford to sit in a room with both alcohol and them. So the pair were at Ford's parents' house the day after his marriage proposal to Tanya was refused yet again. His cousin Geoff received a ringing slap for kissing Tanya under the mistletoe where she had dawdled for too long. Then the poor fool was barely rescued from being beaten senseless by the enraged Ford. In the quiet aftermath, Tanya contentedly sipped rum-laced eggnog while bathing her lifelong friend's abraded knuckles in cold water. Next to him, she could be the second worst bitch forever.

Tell Tales

There went another housekeeper, guided humanely by the elbows as she seemed dazed and disoriented rather than violent. She only mumbled the details of an outlandish-sounding narrative. A hapless young woman, duped despite her graduate degree in psychology — by her crafty elderly employer, a half-blind innkeeper, no less. It was all too preposterous and Gothic for anyone to take the exhausted doctor seriously. She had waited too long to take vacation, perhaps, and the paranoia of her patients had tangled up with reality in her formerly logical mind. The old innkeeper Edna Ella – *"No need to stand on formality here with 'Mrs. Pope'"* – why, she had lived in that old house her entire life.

The Popes had been good people dating back to the turn of the century, when Edna Ella's grandmother and step grandfather, both teachers, had provided a fine, community-serving and arts conscious upbringing for their six children. Only a year and day after headmaster Pope's death, however, Grandmother Pope had married a White man. Edna Ella was the blue-eyed youngest of seven, the "white sheep" of the family as her beautiful, chocolate-hued sisters taunted her. But those three witches, aka the Three Weird Sisters, were dead now, along with Edna's two beloved brothers and That Asshole Harry.

Edna Ella had also buried three husbands. With her school pension and husbands' insurance, she didn't need to make an inn of her ancestral home. She liked the company, and having retired from teaching English and drama at the age of 70, she was happy to indulge in her favorite passion. Edna Ella's Southern-style Sunday brunch kept a steady flow of both short- and long-term "inmates" enlivening the six-bedroom house. Yet the old woman could not hold onto a housekeeper for more than a year or two. Old Auguste the handyman had worked at the Tell-Tale Inn for twenty years. Ligeia the gardener-slash-sous chef was coming up on ten years of employment and 50 years of age. But housekeepers slipped away often and curiously at best, if not tragically.

Daphne had gone for a jog in the woods after weeks of hostile behavior and bizarre claims that Edna Ella had seduced her *man*.

That was, let me think, fifteen years ago, and Edna Ella had indeed been striking at sixty, white hair lightly relaxed into a bob, her bronze skin highlighted by various aquas and teals and mother-of-pearl jewelry. But still! As if she really could have "transfixed" a man with her one good blue-grey eye. Anyhow, poor deluded Daphne had never turned up. Her successor, a hippie watercolorist, had broken a hip and lain at the bottom of the back staircase throughout the night with pockets stuffed full of tiny treasures pilfered from inmates as well as Headmaster Pope's watch. The police shook their heads at the Wharton-worthy villain's insistence that she was being "set up and tripped up" by the tall smirking man whom no one else had ever met. She was carted away in an ambulance, screaming, "Curse your blue eye!"

And now the hapless would-be mental health counselor. Amelie, a pale, frail thing who could have passed for fourteen, in a waifish white dress. Counting her steps between ramblings of "4, 3, 4, 3…." Powders in her tea? The butler spying on her? What butler?! How 19th Century! So paranoid she had even demanded her private food cupboards be padlocked. Edna Ella Pope went back into her house and reached behind the crocheted café curtain to place the sign "Housekeeper Wanted" on the sill. The sign fell, and Edna Ella righted it again, sighing *asshole*. She would definitely be keeping an eye on her next employee.

For Heaven's Sake

If as a girl you coughed in the middle of the night and your mother materialized through the dark with Formula 44, then much later you might as an adult miss her a hell of a lot more than you would be pissed about some annoying quirk of hers that had somehow become part of your inheritance. Thus, nervous and at times exceedingly uptight Jeannie smiled down at the teensy hole in her tights. That miniscule show of flesh would not, for Heaven's sake, drive anyone within eyesight of her 55-year old legs mad with desire. Surely, no one would notice her at all, seated and anonymously sipping at a vanilla latté.

Jeannie straightened her kerchief, worn gypsy style, capping her hair then tied at her nape and dangling down her back like a silk ponytail. It had been her mother's, given to Jeannie in the '90s, some twenty years after her mother had stopped covering her head whenever she left the house. Jeannie's father had "tried on about twenty religions along with a whole slew of hobbies" – Mama had reported – in the thirty years of marriage that preceded his death. The kerchiefs had been in deference to Dad's informal but strict Black Muslim phase; he had tinkered with the Americanized religious and political rules then dubbed his version as the family's code of behavior. The result being that no pork was allowed; his wife wore a kerchief out of doors; and his daughters wore skirts below the knee and their hair was braided down, never allowed to float free, be pressed and uncovered, certainly not afro-styled, etc.

Pulled from her reverie by the arrival of table neighbors, Jeannie suddenly wished a bit angrily that she had stayed home and made biscuits. Only once had she seen Mama's face in a dream in the five years since her mother's death. Mama had been kneading biscuits to go with Jeannie's corn chowder. She liked remembering her parents and sipped angrily at vanilla foam until calmed. Most annoyances could be healed by a warm drink or a long train ride. Jeannie began writing stories about the two giggly girls at the next table.

Jeannie stopped thinking for a moment. Everything around her slowly swirled to a stop too. The girls' lips moved soundlessly. The

28

cash register opened and closed without a *ding*. Even the scritch-scratch of her own pen had vanished. True present was gone. She was 9 and Ted was 7; the siblings sat in the car making up lives for passersby by while their parents attended to grown-up business in the post office. Dad loomed large near the post office doorway. Jeannie could almost hear her mother saying, "For Heaven's sake, they'll be fine for ten minutes, Dear." Like most fathers, Dad thought his children the most beautiful and kidnapworthy offspring on Earth.

Her special daydreams could not be predicted, conjured up, or controlled. Jeannie could see them now very plainly. Mama in her kerchief, brown with burgundy squares and a thin tan border, and a tan-corduroy-collared burgundy barn coat. Sensible dark tan walking shoes with matching tights. Dad was wearing a grey golf cap, snapped in front, dipped just enough to be dapper. Burgundy lines checked across it. In a light blue shirt, without a tie because it was Saturday, wearing burgundy chinos, he still looked like what he was, a former World War II staff sergeant who had migrated to blue-collar Boston after the war and eventually met a girl, settled down finally at 30. Jeannie must have looked dazed, for one of the girls' voices penetrated her vivid flashback to ask if she was okay. Jeannie murmured that she was fine, thank you, but simply could not bear heat. When college kids notice you, you must be looking rough. Jeannie told herself, "Go home to nap, for Heaven's sake."

Touches Knot

As it is always easier to label love foolishness than to categorize one's lack of it a dim, cowardly choice, Xandie rolled her unloving eyes at her friend's news. No, Brenda could not meet the girls for Friday night drinks; she had a second date. Janet smiled and congratulated Brenda. Alex pried for details. Xandie exaggerated her usual dismissive tone to a level of nearly divine superiority that suggested only puny humans engaged in love or lust. Saturday, historically proclaimed, is date night. "What is Mr. Second date doing then?" she snapped.

Brenda was crestfallen. Janet was flabbergasted. Alex was smirking a bit, hoping for some type of drama or fireworks. There were two Alexandra's in the group, complete opposites in personality. To avoid confusion, the mean-spirited Alexandra was called Alex and the callous-to-icy one was Xandie. Janet, the peacekeeper of the group who wanted the best for everyone – on Earth, bless her heart – broke the loveless silence that clung to the air in the wake of Xandie's negativity. Janet asked what Brenda was going to wear.

Everyone has a weak spot. Appropriate clothing was Xandie's. She instantly visualized *the* second date with an orthodontist outfit, formulated a plan for assembling it on a Tuesday night, slapped down a credit card to pay the dinner bill, then whisked the quartet from Fajitas and 'Ritas on West Street to the Boylston Green-Line stop. Shazam! They had bought a flowered skirt, periwinkle sweater (to be worn with exactly one undone pearly white button), and peep-toe patent yellow shoes by the time the Newbury Street and Boylston street shoppes had closed,

They were celebrating loudly by the time Sal del Terre closed. Drunk off margaritas and gourmet grilled cheese, the four friends packed themselves and Brenda's packages into a taxi, zipped down Mass Ave, then West Newton, then Washington, dropping them off one at a time. Until Xandie was a lone passenger. Delirious off the cool night air, she felt the holes in her earlobes, vacated by the pearl drops lent to Brenda, and she fondled the platinum love knot pending between her breasts. The bleak foyer of Xandie's building on Peterborough Street looked even less resplendent than usual. The dark carpet stain seemed larger than before, the faux plants more lifeless; the moody desk attendant was even more rum-soaked and glummer than usual.

Xandie's quartet were all single, yet she walked into the smelly elevator, then the bleak grey hallway, and her pitch-black apartment feeling like the last bachelor in Massachusetts. Was it Plato who wrote: "He whom love touches not lives in darkness"? Xandie realized that nothing at all can touch you if you neglect to reach out. Via computer she had chosen her apartment sight-unseen from Stamford to escape a failing relationship and met her current best friends through a book club. Xandie scrolled through photos of available men on Match.com, mentally scrolling through male faces she saw in person every day. Beginning again felt like everything.

It's Not the Stirring

Kristen stirred her ginger ale in a Long Island Tea glass with a tall, skinny spoon. She was dog sick *and* her arthritis was acting up. Eff physical therapy and yoga. Fifty should not feel the way it felt on her spine any more than size 12 chinos should refuse to glide up over her butt. Man, all that 50 is the new 30 jazzamatazz was undiluted bullcrap. Middle age physically sucked, pure and simple.

Yep, Kristen was a successful women's columnist, just like SJP on *Sex and the City.* And her husband was tall, dark, handsome, and crazy-rich. But her happy and well-settled spirit was getting its big butt kicked by the daily chore of dragging her body the hell around. It was February and Kristen loved February in all its moodily romantic New England glory However, her neck and back and hips and knees and feet – well, they felt like slashing February's freakin' tires.

She swung her now-heavy calves up onto a chair and gulped her ginger ale. She remembered her mother stirring out the carbonation when she was a little kid, so she always had ginger ale when sick. Or sad. Or hungover. Or all of the above.

One day Kristen's husband told her it's not the stirring that really matters. Metal absorbs. It's the metal spoon absorbing the carbonation, not the vortex. Who in hell knew things like that? Well, a scientist.

Kristen read, wrote, watched educational television, and drank tea. She rarely met men who knew a lot of things that she did not. Men who knew things, she befriended or dated. Lenny was so smart that Kristen married him. It wasn't just the romance and corporeal lust for him that mattered. Kristen liked absorbing knowledge.

Nora Wanted the Footlights

Nora wanted the lamplight, the black spiral staircase from a turquoise veranda, and music echoing down a thin, rainy, cobbled street. She did not want to rule the globe, just to be loved by it the way the world loved quirky heroines in romantic comedies and 19th-Century literature. She grew her hair as long as it would go then clipped on extra squiggly romantic curls. Happiness requires cascading curls as well as twirled stairways. But she vowed not to let her story end in the rain. Cold. Trite. Unpleasant.

But Nora could only afford at the age of 53 to rent a basement apartment forty-five minutes away from Copley Square in Boston, the city in which she'd been born. Nora was pragmatic, conservative, and accustomed to poverty. Her salary seemed like a fortune, for she made do with what she could afford, making her life comfortable and colorful albeit deeply lonely. Her new boyfriend Roger held her hand as the two walked toward Nora's apartment building. Apprehension crept alongside their every step.

It was a huge apartment complex in Franklin. The grounds and exteriors were so orderly, pre-fabricated, and uniform that Roger at first felt quite at home. He was from Connecticut. Then the couple of only two months went into Nora's building. They could each feel the other's hesitation. Nora liked Roger yet knew he was a snob. Roger liked Nora but feared her chronic poverty as if it were contagious. They usually hung out at his house, eating take-out lo mein or margarita pizza, watching old black and whites on Turner Classic Movies or playing chess. This would be the first time Roger had seen Nora's home.

The hallway was a dingy yellow brick with alcoves that seemed to be begging to pray to. The carpeting was high-traffic-worthy, of a hue so depressingly neutral as to be un-nameable. Not taupe. Not tan. Not grey. Not beige. They descended the staircase and collectively took a breath as Nora swung open her door. The couch was rough, unvarnished wicker covered with black and scarlet velvet pillows. The rug was bamboo, trimmed black. No coffee table, just red and black wooden bed trays and floor pillows, some with open-faced books, one with a Kindle. Shiny black bookcases had deep red backs inside. One flick had lit the entire room from paper table lanterns, ceiling-hung balloon lights, and two lights almost as tall as Roger. Strings of miniature lamps framed the entrance to the kitchenette and the exit to the terrace on a hill. Roger was enchanted, and Nora was incredulous. Never had it occurred to her that such a privileged man would enjoy her whimsy so enthusiastically. "This is wonderful!" he said, amber-lighted face glowing.

They toted red and yellow silk-corded pillows outside to sit in the wicker wingchairs that Nora had spray-painted teal. Homemade chili with double cornbread from turquoise bowls was apparently food of the gods to Roger. Guest's choice music: Sinatra? Nora wouldn't have thunk it. A bespectacled data clerk who cooked enough food for a platoon, made paper lights, and walked around barefoot on bamboo mats? Who would've guessed? Not Roger. Neither minded the rain stampeding through the trees only four feet away from the concrete walled terrace. Stray splooshes or sprinkles invaded the oasis occasionally. But nothing could touch them.

Useful Things

Ursula would never forget the article in *Cosmopolitan* magazine read during her college years, "Want a man? Be a Bitch." The article explained hissy-fit-throwing, conniving, demanding tactics used by those nasty chicks who always seem to have boyfriends while nice girls sit home with their cats. Ultimately the article had saved desperate Ursula from being a bitch, having sent the message that one might get a man that way yet she would lose herself in the process. Sage, but unfortunately, Ursula did not much like cats.

There were other useful things Ursula had learned from fashion magazines. How to make four scarves, two blouses, a skirt, and two pair of pants into 52 outfits. How to apply clear nail polish to one's nylon stockings to halt a run in its tracks. How to X Band-Aids over nipples so Erin can go braless without looking like a complete hussy. And, most important, when having sex in a coat closet spread his coat wide open, lining side up over the pile first to avoid wool burn. Ursula would have preferred advice on avoiding parties so dull that one must resort to coat-pile sex for entertainment.

Ursula had never got the hang of meeting men that a lusty but sensitive lady would want to get or dupe or seduce into seducing her. Nor could she hold a wineglass by the stem without trepidation. She had problems finding a decent caterer and couldn't, wouldn't bake if you paid her. Worst of all, Ursula was surrounded by 55-year-old single women who had nothing much to speak of other than their manlessness. She thought half these women ought to have mates, since they were complete bitches who had lost themselves decades ago. The other half were dear friends. Most of them didn't have cats. Many of them had gardens and Masters' degrees and wore earthy-crunchy Cambridge women's weeds.

Thad delivered soil the day Ursula went to help her dear friend Jane create a garden in her new yard. Thad's father owned a plant nursery and Thad owned a moving company, so their needs meshed well. Somehow, Thad and his green-thumbed cousin were self-recruited to the procreation of Jane's garden, hiding little peat gnomes of the four of them as they came back weekend after

35

weekend for wine-soaked afternoons of gardening, repaving the drive, cleaning out the garage. Now they've kept that up for eleven years or so. None of them have fallen in love with each other or had sex in closets or elsewhere. Two of them have married and divorced others. They've disagreed and made up. And all four are committed to going out of their way to avoid bitchy people.

Ursula continues to plummet soufflés, sugar wax her legs, date and be temporarily content or instantly disappointed…all while wearing Vixen Plum lipstick. She is just as passionate about owning her own livery fleet, speed walking four miles per day, and volunteer tutoring as ever. She paints very bad watercolors; all that's missing from the lifestyle of her 20s is a feeling of desperation.

Wife, Interrupted

Hester had not married her college boyfriend and moved to Connecticut to procreate at 22, much to the chagrin of her socioeconomically blue collar yet culturally "upper crust" family. The nuclear family had been good people, the children's lives infused with the arts and the importance of formal education for its own sake as well as being presumed a bridge to a middle-class future. But a month into homely Hester's sophomore year toward a better life, her father died and the family framework imploded. A few years later, college freshman Hester met a psycho. Even naïve Hester knew the guy was "off" by the second date. Manners nearly killed her and threw the course of her life off-kilter.

On the second date Hester objected to his language, explained that she intended to finish college and to be a virgin on her wedding night. He could have laughed and left, called her "boring" or "frigid" or "good girl" like kids in high school. Instead, he pretended to respect Hester's choice and see if a strong relationship developed in time. Confused that she was still getting an odd vibe, wanting to get out of the car, Hester hastily agreed to a third date…to say good-bye quite clearly in person. She ended up drugged and bleeding to death, pounding the walls against the deaf ears of neighbors, as she was incapable of reaching the deadbolt. The psycho had casually discussed snacking options, wrapping the phone cord around the tan telephone that he took with him to the store. Hester had blissfully blocked the details for twenty years, but she knew. In and out of consciousness. Nausea. Head throbbing.

Bam! The gurney was rolled through emergency room doors, down very narrow hallways. It was like being launched into space in a coffin. Sound was muffled. Through her tunnel vision caused by impending unconsciousness, Hester saw pure whiteness with angels flying about her. Then the masked face of the surgeon appeared. His eyes were swirled-marble brown and turquoise…and somehow familiar. The doctor's expression assured her that the floating figures were just medical staff rushing in lab coats and light blue scrubs, not angels. If any human could save her, this was the man. A superdoctor at Mass General!

So she had lived. A few years went by. If all had been normal, she would have married her college boyfriend and been a middle-school teacher with an accountant husband in Connecticut. Nice enough. Refined. Handsome and tall. Great catch. But she was damaged, suddenly believing that she deserved to sleep with men she loved for the rest of her life or sleep alone. Not *a* man for life. It was too late for all that; she could not be revirginated. A year after letting go of Mr. Right, Hester fell in love. Then she fell in love. Then she fell in love some more. She loved men. Relished them.

Bam! Fast-forward twenty years. She politely ignored experts who labeled her crazy, merely regretful, spoiled, lying for attention. One voice in the back of Hester's brain outshouted voices outside of herself. One detail emerged and re-emerged though Hester managed to shove the other memories to the back of her mind. If he wasn't a willful criminal, why did he take the phone to the store?

Changeling

Quincy's husband Robb swore he didn't snore, which was odd since he was one of twelve siblings and had grown up Southie Irish poor. Generally, anyone with a whole dang village-worth of siblings has been analyzed half to death throughout his entire adolescence and then some and knows all of his habits, flaws, and quirks — whether he cares to or not — by junior high. Quincy had two sisters and two brothers yet hadn't shared a room since she was eleven and sister number two had bustled off to college. But Quincy knew she bit her nails, also snored, had cartoon dog nightmares, et cetera. Robb had lived in a three-bedroom house, slept on a pull-out sofa with two brothers, perpendicular to a couch full of his two oldest brothers. How in hell could he not know he snored like the Orange Line screeching then grinding in an arc on the el tracks over Washington Street, circa 1976?!

Quincy flapped back the covers to leave the unwitting snorer to his blissful slumber. She was the one who had grown up four blocks from Dudley Station, walked past Dearborn Liquors, El Mondonguito's, the Lot Where the Barber Shop Used to Be, then Brown's Market across the street, and waved to the muscled firemen at "Fort Dudley." Quincy had come from a home with two united-'til-death, strict parents and gone to Boston Latin Academy on the #23 bus. She had excelled in English, History, and Art – sucked at everything else. Robb was the numbers and science mind in the family. The Dennis-Leary-lookalike former high school hockey star. Back then, the pair had only sneaked longing looks at each other.

Quincy checked on her twins on the way to the kitchen. Pearl was snaked around her sheet per usual, one French-pedicured foot dangling off the bed, stark naked with honey-blonde curls obscuring her tan face. She unsmothered her own profile with one deep-wine-polished fingertip, smiled down with her full lips, and tossed a yellow and turquoise flowered quilt over her husband's long form. 30-year reunion? At their 10th, Quincy and Robb had ended up in a room at the Copley Marriott tearing one another's shirts off. Both divorced from ambivalent spouses 5 years later, they had grabbed each other and held on for dear life.

Pearl, at 15, was a breathing emblem of her parents' passion. Every flat surface of her room was covered with stacks of books, Post-It notes sticking out all over. Each wall had a piece of sports equipment propped against it or dangling from a peg. She didn't own a poster or a dress, just turquoise walls and sweats. Robb Jr. rested tidily in his olive and tan, reversible-comforter-tucked room. Nary a book in sight. Computers. Gadgets. Power cords. Vintage board games on metal wall shelving. His snore was less jagged than his father's and his dressing robe matched his camouflage pajamas. Pearl called her curiously black-haired, green-eyed creature of a brother "The Changeling."

Quincy left Robby's door exactly six inches ajar and descended the black and tan staircase to start the coffee. It was 4 a.m. Her family would not stir for another five hours minimum. Quincy assembled an egg, turkey sausage, and hash brown casserole, stuck it in the refrigerator, then baked two dozen apricot-almond muffins, a fourth of which would be brain food for her reading and writing. Forty-eight years on Earth, a successful wedding planner career, and a peculiar yet lovely family. Why should Quincy feel out of place at some silly reunion? She had lived up to her high school nickname, "the hopeless romantic."

The Clank of a Full Wallet

Zora was the coat check girl at Symphony Hall. It was all they would let her do after her latest stint in rehab. No matter what one has or has not done or even been formally accused of, people always assume that drug addicts and drunks are thieves. Zora had drunk and popped away her own money, thank you very much. She was quite proud of her ability to live off of $8.50 per hour. Her tips were amazing. So was the sex. She had met men from all over the city of Boston, from all over the world. Patrons. Funders. Musicians. Ushers. She was an equal opportunity man-loving fool! And men adored and spoiled her back. There were dinners, tickets, limos. Pubs. Basement nightclubs. A condo in Hyde Park. A brownstone on Beacon. Breakfast at the Ritz.

Good thing Zora was off of everything but weed and wine, she thought, eating caviar and laughing at her date's unheard joke. He was gorgeous. Who cared about his dreadful dinner companions: puffer fish Botox bride and Lurch the groom? Zora wanted them to get lost, but somehow the four ended up at the Mandarin Oriental. Lurch made a grab at her so she left. She pick-pocketed her date's weed and five hundreds just because she was pissed at him for passing out.

Zora went to the CVS in Copley Square for Visine and Doritos then hopped a cab back to the pit she shared with three bitches near Lechmere. She flipped off the bitch who huddled in a raggedy-ass navy robe and Hello, Kitty! pajama pants asking where Zora had been. Like some teenaged girl's mother, Eva always demanded answers to which she was 100% unentitled. Screw her. Zora flung two bills at Eva in melodramatic triumph then stomped to her room in stockinged feet.

Then the sun was up and Zora was rested and oddly happy. For maybe ten minutes. Then, there was blood. Lots of it. They were dead. Lurch and his plastic-faced wife. Rich gorgeous dude. All. Slaughtered like pigs. No suspects, just a red-wigged woman in sunglasses on the security camera, not a drop of blood on her. No valuables seemed to be missing except the unpaired man's wedding ring. Gashes. Slashes. Zora snatched the remote from her Asshole

Roommate #2 and turned off the kitchen TV.

Zora felt sick. One of the bitches actually poured her some juice before launching into graphic, shiny-eyed gossip about the red-wigged woman. God, most people were just so horrible and cheap nowadays. Zora had met crackheads more concerned with their fellow humans. But, anyhow, *What the hell, what the hell, what the hell to do?* She couldn't stroll into a police station and tell them what she knew. She could hear the derisive laughter of disbelief...followed by a hollow *clank*!

If It's Yours, It Will Return

Flying is an act of instinct, not the product of intelligence. Thus, the term "bird brain." Silly little creatures pecked prettily at crumbs one moment, sauntered toward the heavens the next. Yet flying was a privilege to Francie, a sacred pact with God to climb higher without getting big-headed about her worthiness of being entrusted with hundreds of human lives on a regular basis.

Francie had first been in a plane at age eight with her neighbor who served as a surrogate father. Everyone called him "Hemingwayne" due to his amazing imagination and experiences harnessed in simple tale-telling. He had been wounded retrieving a fallen comrade in WWII. But Wayne did not exaggerate or brag. He merely laid out the facts with excellent scene-setting ability. The bum arm prevented his becoming a police officer, so he crop-dusted, shouting his biography to passengers.

From the second Francie first set foot in the plane she knew she would be a pilot someday. And she was now the grey-haired, confident, professional figure that posters are made of. She was also going down. For no apparent reason, *goddammit*, and she could not prevent the slow but unintentional descent. Then faster. Faster. Thud. *Screech!* This was it.

And it turned out to be *It* after all. Her first terrible landing. Branches chain-sawed off the cockpit while Francie waited patiently. Jimmy the co-pilot had fainted. Then they were both emerging from the brush to a round of enthusiastic applause and hooting. 351 unscathed passengers were clapping her on the shoulder, calling out, "Good job!" and hugging her. They were naming her a hero.

Francie sat on her Martha's Vineyard front porch sipping rum-laced cider and waving to neighbors. Little kids came over to sit with her, bringing casseroles from their mothers. After work, professionals dropped by to chat a bit, sometimes tucking a quilt around her thighs from the back of the white rattan loveseat that she'd taken to spending most of her days on. Her ex-husband took time off from work to stay with her, managing to coax her indoors when it got chilly at night, have a little fish and her favorite veggie, green beans.

43

Gradually, Francie began to paint, reveling in the hobby she had given up after college. And she made charcoal drawings of all the faces she had seen in her forty-year career. People bought them from the little gallery in town. Francie never thought much about her former work or anything at all. She just watched clouds and let her mind wander, her hand soar, and her husband come back home.

Someone Should Write a Book About This

Laura had tried several careers: college teaching, fashion design, copywriting, online journal publishing, and one storybook-worthy bookstore. She had enjoyed and been damned good at all, but none of it stuck for more than seven years. Laura had also been insanely in love at 25. And at 30. 35 too. Then 40. Laura had passed her unloving 40s as style editor of a New England bride's magazine, longing to be a book publisher and designer instead. Laura had furiously, then halfheartedly begun looking to fall in love again. One perfect Internet-met date had not kissed her goodnight nor followed up on his invitation to a second date. A slightly awkward but sweet enough coffee date had locked her lips in a passionate send-off...then vanished after inviting Laura to dinner. Here she was, ever the freakin' optimist, plodding toward her third first date in three months.

He had seen her profile...and Laura could swear that was him, 6'3" with a Hemingway beard, sitting at the bar. But there was no sign of recognition as Laura stood inside the phone-booth-sized space between the outside door and the inside door. "Old-fashioned Lady Seeks Beautiful Mind." Ladies don't wait at bars, so she certainly couldn't poll the six men sitting at it. Four looked *very* interested, so she was apparently visible and looking right at him.

Had Laura stepped into the pseudo "dive bar" she could maybe see how the meatloaf looked at the table smack in the space where the host would be if Delux were a fine restaurant, a semi-ambient eatery, or even an okay joint for a no-pressure first sip. The place was filling up. After too many "excuse me's" Laura stepped outside into the slight drizzle.

She had spent two hours at a too-long free seminar on independent publishing...for those with money to burn. So Laura waited twenty minutes after the assignated "at the latest" time, shifting tired legs, wanting to cry from the disappointment of the day, hunger, and her embarrassing conspicuousness. Every new laughing group who approached the place ticked her off.

Outside, in the boggy, slow rain, Laura stood on tippy-toe to gaze into the noise-punched, crowded room, envious of the sots with dry-looking fish and white wine that looked like sour grapes juice in the dim.   Laura became infuriated by the tall stranger at the bar. Bearded in maybe, he glanced interest yet neither smiled nor budged. It began to pour. Laura dragged her galoshes to Back Bay Station, shaking with hunger and dejected that the day showed quite clearly she would never be a working artist nor a noted publisher, just some odd duck in between.

Go East, Old Woman!

The drum said, "Go left." Isis kept going left as the ski instructor screamed for her to turn right. She had soared down the mountain — feet disappearing, body feather-light, cold air kissing her face until all she felt was the warmth of the sun lifting her skyward. If Isis turned right she would fall down. Her friend Laverne joked that she was too unconventional to ever go right.

Isis spent eight hours pigeon-toeing up the hill because no way in hell she was getting on that kray-kray ski lift. Isis spent eight hours flying then falling. Isis spent eight hours burning through six ski instructors' vain attempts to teach her to ski. But Isis did not learn to turn right yet again.

Twenty-two years in California and another eight in Dallas had sent Isis the same message: Go live in the postcard towns of New England. She was an adwoman in Boston, the best. She spent every weekend and vacation trying something athletic and New Englandy. Isis sucked at athletic. Isis sucked at cold weather. She'd nearly drowned taking parasailing lessons on the Charles River. She caught every cold or flu bug that winked at her. She got frostbite on two toes on a camping and lake-skiing trip.

Everyone Isis met told her she should take up knitting or reading or making beer. Anything nice and safe and indoorsy. Nature was not for her, her Native American ancestors notwithstanding. But, finally, Isis had discovered what she'd come for. She was prepared to fulfill her purpose.

For twenty-five years since moving East, she had completed everything on her list. At sixty-five, she was by all accounts living a successful life. Now Isis heard the drum getting louder. She tucked her arms, squatting into her maximum speed ever. Her brown eyes clung to the air before her until two grey eyes locked onto her gaze. And the white wolf dashed left, disappearing into a thicket of trees. Isis smiled, closed her eyes, and swerved left.

Failure to Thrive

Opal lived in the projects. She had a "personality disorder" and her family had died or abandoned her. Except, her daughter had gone away to college; she'd seen to that. Opal's ex-husband was an attorney. He had fought over everything: the house, both cars and the SUV, each vase…until Opal just gave up. She had walked out of her marital home of thirty years, leaving the keys in the mailbox.

She had walked into the homeless shelter services with nothing but a month's Charlie Card and a small tote bag. They were bused, like criminals, to the shelter where she was "housed" for two years. Her lone fat suitcase on wheels and laptop stayed in her best girlfriend's guest room. For two years Opal lived at the shelter nights, zapped on double doses of Xanax.   Days she lived in Coraline's huge, empty house. She showered and changed into a different long-sleeved tee shirt and pair of stretchy charcoal leggings. She ate leftovers and watched the Oxygen Channel, watched hundreds of husbands slaughtered in some ghastly fashion by wives who had *Snapped*. Then she would nap, put on her hoodie, and walk almost on her toes from the drugs to Waban, taking the D line from Waban to Park Street, the Red Line to Central Square to her SRO at the Y. SRO.   That's what it was called when one was lucky enough or crazy enough to get a private "cell" instead of being in one of the larger shelters…"in the general population" as it were.

Then her name just popped to the top of some list, and Opal moved to a disabled and elderly apartment complex on Mass Ave in Cambridge. Having her own home, with a living room and a tiny terrace covered with pansies and begonias, a yellow sofa bed – her housewarming present from Coraline – and new friends from art class who came over for poker Friday nights…. All of it was more of a shock to her system than being abandoned, having mental health "episodes", and being homeless had been. She was thriving from contentment. No one had ever taught her to be content, much less happy. Her family had been eternally useful and impressive. She had been just a very good wife and mother, an underachiever for her generation's standards.

Opal was petrified of having her little world snatched away. She sat

48

up 'til dawn, partly because of the weaning down to lower dosages of medication, partly because she was on the look out for her own personal grim reaper. The luxury of borrowing Coraline's life had been a fantasy on Earth. Now that napping afternoons was normalized, it was harder to trust. And friends? Watercolors, for chrissake?

Opal was not supposed to live. From the very beginning. Low weight at birth and refusing to eat, her prognosis had been grim. The hospital had sent he mother home before naming her. Baby Girl, Failure to Thrive. But her father had come every day, and Opal had taken the bottle from him, and she had lived since then with very low expectations. Not smart or pretty or memorable in any way. Few but close friends. No dates. Just a girl who could draw, paint, work magic with clay. An art scholarship and internship had landed her in the line of vision of Boston's elite at the gallery on Newbury Street. That's where she'd caught Stephen's eye and left her future to join his. But that was a long time ago. Now, all that was left was art and friendship.

Hexagon

Yoyo was finally back in Massachusetts. She got a job in a small boutique in Faneuil Hall. She sold a lot of hand-painted goods for outrageous prices. Tourists loved Miss Yolanda's tales about New England. She was like a human encyclopedia on the topic. At 18 she had gone to college in Vermont then moved to Rhode Island until she was 25, married to her old college boyfriend Neill who looked a lot like President Obama only with milk chocolate brown skin and, for too long, a skinny mustache.

At 30, Yoyo had remarried and moved to Mystic, Connecticut with her Master's degree in Sociology and prize roses. Her apple-berry lattice topped pie was legendary. Her two daughters and son adored her. She and her husband, with zero animosity, ignored each other from separate double beds in the same master suite. Dex slept from 10pm to 6am. Yoyo sat up until 2, writing journal entries worthy of John Boy Walton in local color and detail.

At 50, Yoyo was divorced and attending graduations galore, leaving her son with his father, being the cool mom on college visits to her daughters. She weeded her book collection down to 2,000 to tote to New Hampshire University for a PhD in Composition. Yoyo learned to ski, snowshoe, and win archery tournaments while teaching at her alma mater and selling lesson plans on the Internet.

At 55, Yoyo spent one year in Vermont churning butter and joining co-ops while teaching online courses. She moved to Maine, entertaining her grandchildren and neighbors in a huge red converted barn, her one-room home with a loft bed that saw plenty of company too. That lasted for ten years alongside her fame as a local color novelist.

So at 65, Yoyo worked part-time at the Embellish store, researching her next book, and went home to her children who had bought a lovely puddingstone-porched house in Washington Square in Brookline. The house was bursting with spouses, children, friends, neighbors. Yoyo enjoyed being the life of every party, reciting the tales of Edgar Allan Poe from memory over spiked punch or eggnog at home, revealing her own stories one chapter at a time with a significant number of non-retirees at the Purple Parrot Tavern on Fridays. Most of all, however, Yoyo relished commuting to and from her day job, writing drafts in pen and ink on the pale blue lines of her journals. This gloomy, rain-soaked evening she penned: "Gretchen wrote tiny stories...."

~

Author's Bio and Photo

Photo by Todd Collins, Somerville, MA - Autumn, 2015

Mignon Ariel King was born in Boston's City Hospital in 1964. She graduated from Girls' Latin School/Boston Latin Academy. King holds a Master of Arts in English degree from Simmons College. She is the publisher of Hidden Charm Press (which publishes the online journal *MoJo!*) and of Tell-Tale Chapbooks.

Ms. King has been reading at open mics since 1998, sometimes singing '70s Hard Rock tunes. Her autobiographical pentalogy, written in three genres from 1996-2010, is based on a lifetime spent in Greater Boston as a third-generation New Englander and former teacher. King identifies as a womanist.

See the blog *Making Books* (www.mignonarielking.wordpress.com) for more information, or send an e-mail to making2@outlook.com.

~